BEDTIME STORI

RUSSELL SMEAT

@tikirussy

Originally funded through Kickstarter

A digital version is available

Printed in the United Kingdom

Printed by Quoin Publishing

Design: Marcus Diamond

@mrmarcusdiamond

Contents

01 Monday Morning

Monday morning and Richard was the first one in the office.

He'd cycled into work and switched his computer on still in his sweaty cycle shorts. He gazed out of the window, high up in the tower where he worked. Dark clouds gathered, and the atmosphere felt cold and damp.

Fucking typical Monday—he was going to get soaked going home. He sighed, turned back to his computer and logged onto Facebook. Nothing much going on. Izabela, the intern, still hadn't accepted his friend request and today was the last day of the internship program. This was shaping up to a typically shitty Monday. It was only 9am and already things were crap.

Mood as black as his cold coffee, he glanced at the clock. Surely the others should be here by now. They were cutting it fine if they wanted to be at the meeting on time. He ambled out of his office into the open area and made himself a fresh coffee. Burning his lips on his hot drink, he stumbled, spilling coffee down his cycling top, glad there was no one around to see him. Looking around, he wondered why the place was so dead. Sure, it was Monday morning. No one liked going to work on Monday. But the meeting was a big one. Where were they? Time was ticking by, and the boss would be really pissed off if they were late.

Sod it, he wasn't going to get into trouble. He'd go down to the meeting alone if he had to. He got changed into his work clothes and headed off to the boardroom.

The boardroom was rumoured to be an old war bunker, built during World War II. Presumably it had been constructed before the main tower as the elevator didn't go down that far. The only way to get to it was down a cascade of slippery, worn steps. As he descended, the temperature started to drop to a cold clammy level. Weak bulbs overhead were protected with slightly rusted wire, casting spider-like shadows down the stairwell. As he descended, the only sound was his footsteps clattering loudly into the darkness.

The lights started to flicker and fizz. As he fumbled in his pocket for his phone he was suddenly grasped on both arms and violently pushed forward. His heart thumped into his mouth, and stomach filled with ice as something cold and wet slid into his ear. He screamed, curling up into a foetus-like ball. A bright flash went off followed by raucous laughter and a ragged shout of 'wet willy!'

'Oh you twats!' he laughed as he saw his work colleagues, heartbeat still running away down the stairs.

'Dude, you should have seen your face!' Said one of his colleagues, slapping him on the back.

'Ha, you have to check out this picture! That's definitely going on Facebook,' said another, passing his phone around showing a balled-up Richard, hugging himself in fear. Laughing, they tumbled into the boardroom. The tension in the room was so thick it stopped them dead in their tracks. The boss was already there glaring at them from the head of the table. With downcast eyes they quickly took their places.

The room became deadly silent.

A bell chimed and Richard took his cue. He stood up and started the chant. From around the table the others joined in the ancient sounds of the lost language. Incense coiled oily around the corners of the room. The Boss stood up and his massive toad-like bulk was visible to all.

His naked, warty belly glistened with drool dribbling from his mouth as his tongue lolled out, large enough to lick his navel. His eyes changed from angry to hungry.

The chanting reached its climax, a trapdoor opened in the ceiling and a screaming intern crunched onto the large table. For such a large bulk, the boss was remarkably quick and the crumpled body was devoured in seconds, leaving behind a spray of blood and gristle.

Several interns later, the meeting was over and everyone headed back to their office cubicles.

Richard disrobed and wiped the dried blood and gore from his face with a tissue. He logged into Facebook and shook his head to see a video of himself practically crapping himself, gathering likes and comments.

Seriously, could this Monday get any worse? His computer pinged, FFS, what now? Not for the first time that day, his heart skipped a beat.

Izabela, the intern, had accepted his friend request. Seconds later his computer pinged again as an email popped into his inbox.

> Hi Rich,

> Great news! I was made a permanent member of staff today.

> Be prepared to see a lot more of me!

> Izabela x

That x after her name made him smile, as did the fact that she hadn't been eaten. Seconds later, another email came through.
This time from the boss.

> Richard,

> Good meeting. It went well. We need more interns though.

>This time make them young. I have terrible indigestion.

> N

Whoa! Grinning stupidly, he sat back on his chair, looking out the window. The clouds had gone, leaving a clear blue sky. The meeting had indeed gone well. It looked like the Old Ones had been thwarted one more time. This Monday had taken a serious turn for the good. The world wasn't going to end (just yet), the boss had personally emailed him and Izabela had accepted his friend request (oh, and was still alive). All said and done, Rich decided Mondays weren't so bad after all.

02 Snot

My eyes are itchy, my nose is bunged up and I'm forever sneezing. Don't get me wrong—I love summer. I'm just sick of hay-fever.

Judging by the amount of red eyes and sniffing in the office, I'm not the only one suffering.

The weather forecast last night reported that there would be even higher pollen counts. I've stockpiled a load of nose spray. I'll be fine.

Another day over, another bucket of snot. The office was half empty today. Several called in sick, but some we didn't hear from at all. Not even an email.

When I got home I had a crazy sneezing fit. I hawked up a great glob of snot. That wasn't too bad. What was bad was the creature squirming inside. It looked like a foetus or a shrimp. I flushed it down the toilet before puking. Maybe I was mistaken. I mean, it makes no sense, right?

My skin still crawls thinking about it.

Waking up this morning, I couldn't breathe. My nose was totally blocked. I didn't sleep well either. Dreams of that snot-thing kept waking me. I tried to call in sick, but no-one picked up so I just sent an email.

I sneezed out another one of those things. Don't ask me why, but I've put it in a jar. I guess I wanted to prove I'm not going crazy. The thing flopped about pathetically until I filled the jar with water. Now it's swimming around. It looks a bit like one of those Sea Monkeys. You know, the ones that look cute on the picture but are just fleas or something?

I wonder if I should feed it. It comes to the jar wall when I tap it. The weather forecast says the pollen count tomorrow is going to reach record levels. I've ran out of nose-spray, and my nose is locked solid with mucus.

Every time I blow it another creature slithers out. I know it's not normal but that's what happens. I've been putting them in the jar with the first one but it eats them, growing rapidly. As it grows 'it' is becoming a 'she', and she is beautiful.

This morning I was woken by a smashing sound. She had somehow fallen off the shelf, shattering her jar. As I came into the kitchen she sat in a puddle of broken glass and water, pleading at me with those gorgeous eyes.

There was no weather forecast today, only static from the radio. I've not seen or heard from anyone in a while. It's just her and me. She continues to grow so I've moved her into the bath. When I touch the water, visions fill my head of a place that is not on Earth. It's the most beautiful, relaxing place I've ever seen. Unknown stars swirl in an indigo sky and all around is warm blue water. It's just her and me forever.

She keeps inviting me to get into the bath.

Tonight I'll join her.

03 Balls

On the last day of humanity, Dave and Paul were travelling across the Pennines. A light rain slicked the roads, mist slowly creeping down from the hills. Conversation inside the car had lulled to a brotherly silence, the only sounds being the swish of windscreen wipers and the hum of the engine.

'I do believe I've got to drop the kids off,' announced Paul, breaking first the silence and then wind to prove his point. Dave wound down the window and dutifully pulled into the next petrol station they came to.

Paul headed off to find a toilet; Dave went to fill up the car.

'Mate!' Paul shouted across the parking lot, 'I need you to come and stand by the door. There's no lock!'

‘Alright,’ sighed Dave ambling over, ‘but be quick. I don’t want to look like a pervert or something.’

‘Too late for that, bender,’ Paul grinned and closed the door behind him.

Minutes later Dave heard a loud splash from inside.

‘Dude! Courtesy flush,’ laughed Dave, but to no reply. Minutes passed, silent but for the increasing patter of rain. Dave knocked, calling out to his brother. Still no reply. Frowning, he gently pushed open the door and peered inside. The room was empty except for a buzzing fly and a single bulb casting flickering light. Frown deepening, he edged into the toilet and checked behind the door but Paul was nowhere to be seen. As Dave stood, scratching his head, he spotted the large metal ball in the toilet bowl. Walking slowly to the toilet, Dave bent down to get a closer look. It was smooth apart from what looked like a red button.

Underneath the button he could just make out some writing obscured by the toilet water. After one last look around, Dave picked it up and dried it with tissue. The writing said:

PAUL NOBLE
23·1·1974
BASS PLAYER

Scalp itching, Dave stood up, confused. Still expecting Paul to jump out from some hidden spot, he left the room, cradling the metal sphere, and went into the petrol station. Empty and silent, apart from the gentle tapping of rain. He peered behind the counter and there were two metal balls, identical to the one he was carrying. Both had a red button and inscriptions:

KEITH JONES
4·9·1956
ADULTERER

SAMANTHA BENNETT
14·3·1984
ATTENDANT

His head spun. Wondering if this was some elaborate joke, he looked around to see if there was a hidden camera crew waiting to pounce.

Pressing the red button did nothing. He shook the ball but it was silent.

Taking out his mobile phone he rang home. There was no answer, and Dave felt ice freeze his stomach and crawl up his spine.

In a daze, Dave left the building. There was another car he'd not noticed previously at the pumps. As he walked over through the increasing rain he fought the urge to run. His heart sank when he spotted another ball in the driver's seat.

LESLEY CARTER
11·7·1971
DOCTOR

Shoulders sagging, Dave went back to his car and slumped into the driver's seat. He carefully placed the ball with his brother's name on the passenger seat. Tears threatened to burst free as his throat thickened.

None of this made any sense. After staring blankly out the window Dave started the car up. The rain was coming down harder now. His mind raced and skittered inside his head. It felt like he'd drank too much coffee, his brain refusing to sit still and process what was happening.

The only thing he could think of was home. Back to his Mum and Dad, back to cups of tea, toast, and fluffy towels. Back where life was normal.

He pulled out of the petrol station. As he drove back the way he and his brother had just come, Dave's last thoughts were about his family.

Seconds later, the car veered off the road, crashing into a small bank.

Two metal balls rolled out of the wreckage. They bounced and clanked down a hill before finally coming to rest in a mossy gully.

-

Time passed. The earth rotated around the sun. With no humans left, buildings quickly decayed, choked by ivy. Roads crumbled and cracked.

Cultivated fields became overgrown with weeds and livestock were eaten by ever wilder wildlife. Dogs moped after missing owners before eventually forming savage packs. Cats instantly reverted back to their natural feral state and prospered. Forests once more reclaimed England and the air became dense as spores spurted into the ether, unchecked by humanity.

Metal spheres littered the world. Some were buried in the collapsed entrails of houses. Others lay on the ocean floor, submerged in the rusting carcasses of crashed airplanes. A few escaped unscathed, and lay glinting in the sunshine.

-

Exactly one million years later the red button on Dave's sphere started to flash. A squirrel shuffled up, attracted by the flashing light. Evolution had thrust the creature up the food chain. They were no longer the cute furry animals of the 21st Century. The common squirrel now reached just over a meter tall, covered in thick fur with large canine teeth. It picked up the sphere, shaking it, accidentally pressing the flashing button as it did so.

Blinding light erupted from the ball causing the squirrel to run for cover. Seconds later the light subsided, and there stood Dave. He rubbed bleary eyes and looked around. The first thing he saw was the squirrel, staring with hungry eyes as drool dripped from its snarling maw. Panic rooted Dave to the spot. The squirrel crouched, all the while

staring at Dave. Dave was no expert, but that crouch looked like the squirrel was getting ready to pounce. Instinct kicked in, telling him not to break eye
contact, and he slowly stepped back, tripping over a shiny ball as he did.

The squirrel stood up, head cocked to one side, as Dave floundered on the floor. As he squirmed in the mud his attention was momentarily taken by the flashing light on the ball. Without thinking he slammed the button down, white light exploding from the ball. After his eyes recovered there stood his brother Paul, as if he'd never been away.

The squirrel had seen enough and ran, leaving the brothers to reunite.

They stood facing each other for a moment before hugging. At once, they both started talking, bursting out with laughter. Neither could explain. The last thing Paul remembered was going to the toilet, and that was that. Dave remembered seeing the shiny balls, remembered setting off for home, and then nothing. Neither had any answers, only questions. As they looked around the questions only increased. Where was the road? Where was the petrol station? What the hell was that thing just now?

With nothing else to do, they decided to walk up the nearest hill, maybe try and recognize some landmarks. The long, dense grass made the going tough and soon they were huffing and puffing. Unseen things scurried away as they stomped up the hill. As they climbed they spotted an outline of what might have been a building. Exchanging glances, they strode towards it. As they got nearer they could see several flashing red lights.

The brothers collected a total of three balls together. The three that Dave had seen in what seemed like another life: Keith (the adulterer); Samantha (the attendant) and Lesley (the doctor).

'You know,' started Dave hesitantly, 'there was one of these balls with your name on it.'

'You what?'

'I dunno…I mean, when I pressed that button there was this flash of light and there you were,' replied Dave. They both looked at the three balls, brows furrowed. After a moment, Paul shrugged and walked up to the ball with Keith's name on it. Picking it up, he was about to press the button when Dave stopped him with a cough.

Frowning, Paul looked over at his brother who shook his head in way of response. Neither said a word as Paul's hand hovered over the flashing button. Slowly Paul's hand moved away from the button. He gently put the ball back down next to the others and moved away, as though the balls were bombs, about to explode.

As soon as the ball was back with the others the brothers started babbling to each other. Did they want an adulterer with them? Maybe just the doctor? Why not the attendant? Was an adulterer a bad person?

Backwards and forwards they went, conversation rattling round and round as the sun started to go down.

A light wind picked up, cooling their sweat and rippling the grass like the sea. A bird tweeted overhead as insects chirped, hidden in the green ocean. In the dying light Dave looked at over the fields. In all directions he could see flicking lights, like swarms of fireflies. It took a minute or two to register they were in fact the flashing lights of more balls — thousands of them, stretching out in the distance.

Turning to at his brother, he could see that Paul had also noticed the flashes, mouth open. Closing his mouth, Paul turned slowly to Dave and said with a sigh 'Oh balls'.

04 The Street

The creature stirred in its nest. Something was dragging it into wakefulness. It tried to scrabble back into the foetid warmth of its den, back to the black oblivion of sleep. Alas the summoning was too strong, too powerful and it had no choice but to surface. It pushed out into the open and tasted salt in the cold damp air. Picking the slugs off its skin, it growled angrily. This was not the time for it to be awake but it couldn't resist the call. Slowly, with creaking limbs, it moved towards the summoning.

The Street was long and curved, nestled in a quiet and leafy suburb.

Behind the houses was light woodland which backed onto soft rolling hills. The North East coast was a short walk away, and the frequent mists carried with them the faint taint of the sea.

On that October evening, the street was alive with kids laughing and shouting at each other. A light mist was starting to settle, making Halloween even more atmospheric than just the approaching gloom.

As the kids gathered in their gangs, the excitement grew and people got ready for the night's entertainment.

Most of the people living on the street were prepared for Halloween.

Looking down the street showed a patchwork of light and dark. Some houses were pitch black, their inhabitants hiding behind closed curtains, waiting for the night to be over. However a good proportion of the houses were lit and decorated. The unwritten rule was that if there were decorations on display it was okay to knock there. Those were the ones that would welcome the gaggles of trick or treaters.

The kids had a good idea of where to go. They exchanged tips with each other as to the best places to visit. There were The Barlows. An older couple with no kids, they loved Halloween. The kids knew that this was a sure thing for a good haul. Another house was at the opposite end of the street—Old Lady Jones. She was generally regarded as harmlessly crazy due to her belief that every day was Easter. The kids knew that she was sure to dish out chocolate eggs and that was just fine. In the middle of the street was The Flash Guy. He smiled too much with his mouth, never his eyes. The trick or treaters would most likely be avoiding his house. Over the road from him was The Loner. He kept to himself but seemed safe enough. He didn't say much but was okay about returning stray balls that got kicked into his garden. And so it went.

Dave had arranged for everyone to meet outside his house. He checked his watch. 7pm. Almost everyone was there. He took a quick look at his gang. Unfortunately Adrian had showed up even though he was too old to go trick or treating. Adrian was showing off his collection of rotten eggs. He said he was going to throw them at houses that didn't give them sweets. Dave frowned. He didn't want the night to be spoiled by some shitty eggs. Besides he hoped Felicity would turn up. Felicity had moved in opposite him at Number 25 a few months back. Whilst he would never admit it to the gang he really fancied her. She dressed a bit odd and had dyed hair which had gotten her the nickname Goth Girl but he didn't care. She was the prettiest girl he'd ever seen. He'd bumped into her the other day and had tried to play it cool. He had mumbled something about how a bunch of them were going to go trick or treating tonight.

As his watch ticked the butterflies in his stomach kicked it up a notch.

Was she going to turn up? Wasn't she?

At 7.10pm everyone was getting restless. He couldn't stall things any longer. It was clear she wasn't going to turn up. He gave one last look towards her house and tried to shrug it off, tried not to show his disappointment. He cursed his mumblings. Sod it, time to get some sweets. Halloween was officially on!

Felicity watched from her bedroom, peeking out behind the curtains.

She wanted to go with them. The leader (was his name Dave? David?) seemed nice. He had almost ran over her at school and had blurted out about they were going out tonight. Her parents had even said she could go if she wanted. But she was still new to the area and he hadn't actually invited her out. As she watched the gang disappearing into the thickening mist she convinced herself that she didn't really want to go.

Maybe next year. She turned away from the curtain and opened her book, vaguely annoyed at herself.

The Barlows were ready for the kids. They didn't have any kids of their own. They had decided to focus on their careers first and do the kids thing later. Unfortunately now it was too late. Mrs. Barlow had been told by the doctors she couldn't conceive. Now they lived a quiet life, enjoying the sounds of the kids in the street having fun. Halloween was a bitter-sweet day for them. They loved the chance to play, but it made them sad that it would never be their children going trick or treating.

Still, they were ready. The pumpkin was in the window with its candle lit, the plastic skull was filled with goodies and Mr. Barlow had even put up a fake spider on the door. As the doorbell rang for the first time that evening The Barlows looked at each other with sad smiles before opening the door.

The creature felt the summoning pull at its bones. It followed the calling to a large garden where it found small animals that had been prepared, carefully crucified on small wooden crosses. It quickly devoured them, throwing the skins away as it crunched through bone and gristle.

Wiping blood and fur from its maw, it moved towards the house from where the summoning emanated. With one hunger quenched the creature felt more awake, but now it felt another hunger rise—quite literally.

Barry sat waiting for the knock on his door. He had really gone to town this year. Not one but two pumpkins, spiders sitting in webs, even a fake cauldron filled with sweets. As he sat in his front room he indulged himself with fantasies about the kids walking past. He hoped that new girl with the purple hair would come knocking. She could show him a few tricks he was sure. His fantasies became more fervid as he pictured a steamy scene involving the new girl and some of the other little teases he'd kept an eye on over the past month or so. Any minute now there would be that knock and oh, was he ready.

Mike had promised himself a quick 10 minute break from writing what was certainly going to be his best-seller. 10 minutes had turned into two online arguments with random strangers and now he sat refreshing his screen, waiting impatiently for responses to his latest scathing comments.

Eyes aching, he wondered if he should get up and do something else. A knock at his door provided the perfect excuse to move. As he headed towards his door Mike remembered today was Halloween. Thinking fast, he took the box of chocolates from on top of the fridge and emptied them into a plastic bowl. A bit old, but better than nothing. A chorus of 'Trick or Treat!' Greeted him and he felt himself grin as childhood memories came flooding back.

The gang was moving down the street, pulling in a fine trawl of sweets.

The Barlows had been perfect, just as they'd expected. Dave had suggested they try The Loner and he had also come up gold. Still no sign of Felicity, but a sugar rush from a few sneaky nibbles had cheered Dave up. Maybe he should keep some sweets and give some to her?

His stomach flipped again at the thought of her face and he smiled to himself. Tonight was a good night. The gang unanimously decided to avoid The Flash Guy and they continued down the street.

Old Lady Jones was getting ready in her own way. She'd stocked up on chocolate eggs. Her failing memory struggled to understand why kids came knocking at her door but she didn't mind. They loved the eggs and that was all that mattered. As she arranged the eggs in the basket she continued the chanting that brought the beast closer. As she opened the door the smell of it almost bowled her over; dank like an old cellar that contained several dead goats. She put on the rubber gloves. This part of the ritual wasn't going to be pleasant.

The beast was at the door of the house. The call promised release from his desire. The door opened and the human stood there. He presented himself for the cleansing and the human provided the necessary rituals.

The seed was collected in a large jar. Warm and thick, smelling of dead fish and lavender it filled the jar to the brim. Ritual complete, the door was shut and the beast was free to go.

Old Lady Jones used the contents of the jar to glaze the chocolate eggs. She mixed in some vanilla essence to remove the fishy stench and coated the eggs with a thick sheen. By the time she had finished, the smell had all but gone and the glaze had dried. A few minutes later a knock on the door signalled the arrival of the first batch of kids. She smiled to herself and got her basket of eggs ready.

No one had knocked on Barry's door. He had dredged through a variety of depraved websites to pass the time. This had naturally led to a vigorous masturbation set to fantasies involving most of the little cock teases of the street. Session finished he now felt unclean, depressed and lonely. There was only one cure. A bath so hot it would almost burn away his guilt and make him clean again. He switched off the downstairs lights and went upstairs to run the water.

Outside the mist continued getting thicker, muffling sounds and making for a perfect Halloween. The street lights became yellow balls glowing as the night got darker. To Dave's horror the gang decided to try Goth Girl's house. His heart jumped into his mouth as they got closer. He half-heartedly suggested they call it a night as the mist threatened to become rain. After some jeering he shut up and so there they were, at the bottom of the path that led up to Felicity's house. For the first time that night he hung back as someone else rang the door. He watched with pounding heart as the door opened. It wasn't Felicity but her Dad.

He smiled at them and offered up a large bowl of sweets. After the gang had taken their fill, Dave loitered in the doorway as a crazy idea came to him.

'Can I help you?' Asked her Dad in a kind voice. Dave swallowed. As a future father-in-law, he sounded pretty cool. Dave shuffled his feet a bit and then brought out one of the eggs from Old Lady Jones.

'Erm, could you…er…give this to Felicity please?' stammered Dave, mouth so dry it felt like he was clicking rather than saying words.

He thrust the egg into Felicity's Dad's hands and ran down the path after the gang. As he sprinted down the path he heard Felicity's Dad calling for her as the door gently shut behind him. Barely able to contain his smile he leapt over the fence as adrenalin surged through his body. This was proving to be the best night ever!

Slowly but surely the night was coming to an end. The stream of door knockings had died down to a trickle and The Barlows knew that Halloween was over. Mrs. Barlow put away the few remaining sweets.

As she looked down at the empty plastic skull she felt tears swell up.

Rather than cry in front of her husband she took herself outside round the back of the house. The mist obscured the trees at the back and made everything still. A rustling sound made her start. Before she could react in any way the beast loomed out of the mist. He was still not finished with the night. The ritual had been completed but his body still pulsed and ticked with energy. He could smell the human, and he liked what he could smell. Shortly after a slightly dishevelled Mrs. Barlow came back indoors. Her husband looked questioningly at her muddy knees.

She brushed it off, saying she's slipped at the back of the garden and yes she was fine, no need to fuss. She threw her dirty clothes in the laundry basket and stepped into a steaming shower, not entirely sure what had just happened. Despite the scratches and bruises she felt oddly satisfied.

Her stomach seemed full and she rubbed her tummy in the shower, smiling down at her navel.

Felicity had taken the egg from her Dad who had tried to explain who had dropped it off. Even now she couldn't stop herself smiling. From her Dads description she knew it was Dave. She sat in her bedroom studying the egg. Nothing too unusual, apart from it wasn't Easter. She unwrapped and cracked open the chocolate egg and started to nibble at the edges. Finding it delicious, she quickly devoured it. The warm afterglow of chocolate made her calm so she said her good nights and climbed into bed, still smiling to herself. For the first time since arriving in the street, she was looking forward to going to school.

Adrian was bored. Everyone was starting to go home in dribs and drabs.
There was no way he was going to end the night without throwing his rotten eggs at something. He had carried those stupid things all night and now his hands stank. As he walked home he noticed the lights had gone out at Flash Guys' house. Perfect. No one liked that twat anyway.

Adrian hurled the eggs at the front window. Splat! Bullseye! The eggs burst with a sulphuric stench that he could smell from the street. He ran away quickly, laughing to himself. As Adrian ran he noticed Old Lady Jones still had her lights on and he quite fancied some more of her chocolate eggs. He decided one last call was in order before home time.

Mike scoffed the last remaining chocolates as he demolished the online idiots once and for all. He now sat looking at a blank document, words failing to make his best seller. Maybe a cigarette would help relax his mind, get the creativity flowing. Mike stepped out the back of the house, preferring to smoke in the garden whilst listening to the trees swish in the wind. The mist was really thick now and there was no breeze to stir the air. He could just about make out the trees at the back, draped in fog. As he lit a cigarette a scuffling noise from the bottom of the garden made him jump. He stamped out his barely smoked cigarette and went back inside the house, locking the door behind him. Maybe it was time to call it a night. He switched off the computer and headed to bed. His best seller would wait another day.

The beast watched from the woods as Mike went back inside his house and growled quietly in frustration. Despite his encounter with Mrs. Barlow, he still wasn't ready to go back to hibernation. There was still a few drops of hunger within him that needed shedding. He headed back the way he had come, back to where he had been summoned.

Maybe the human there would service him one last time before he crawled back into his hole to finish his sleep.

Dave and the other kids were all safely home. The night had been a great success. The chocolate eggs from Old Lady Jones were so tasty, every kid had eaten at least one before going home. Now, as the night drew to an end, Dave sat in bed. He couldn't resist munching on one last egg. His teeth were aching after all the sugar but they were just too tasty. Being a good boy he went to the bathroom to brush his teeth. As he stood brushing he replayed the night and felt himself smiling at the memory of handing over the egg to Felicity's Dad. The butterflies in his stomach still fluttered about but they were settling down to dream and soon so would he.

Adrian couldn't get any answer from Old Lady Jones. Just as he was about to go home he heard a noise round the back, probably the old bag herself. Maybe if he asked her nicely she would give him some more of those eggs. He pushed the gate open and walked down the path.

Peering through the thick mist he could just about see her, hunched over something. As he got closer he realised his mistake. It was not Old Jones.

As it stood up to face him it was big—much bigger than Mrs. Jones. It was also pink and shiny. The mist obscured his view, but it looked as though its skin was inside out or something. As Adrian stood there, rooted to the spot, more details were revealed as it stepped closer. Its head was massive, with huge jaws slobbering drool that hissed onto the ground.

The thing had large pointed ears and to Adrian it somehow looked like a huge skinned rabbit. The last thing Adrian saw before blacking out was its huge member jutting towards him. Mercifully he lost consciousness as the creature casually flipped him over before releasing its last remnants of desire.

The next few days in the street were chaotic. Adrian regained consciousness in the early hours of the morning and had limped home, bleeding and sore. He tried to keep it a secret but the stained underpants and bloody towels told his parents that something seriously wrong had happened. The police were called in and a door to door enquiry began. It wasn't long after that Barry's corpse was found sitting silently upstairs in the bath. The blood from his slit wrists had long ago cooled and congealed. A quick search of his property revealed his vast array of child pornography, alongside a collection of stolen underwear.

As no suicide note was found a full police investigation was instigated.

The street was never the same again. Felicity's parents quickly sold their house and moved far away from the street. Dave was sad, heartbroken even, but he understood their reasons—what with the police and press, the street had become a bit like a circus. Old Lady Jones became a minor celebrity for a time: she was nicknamed the Easter Lady as she handed out Easter eggs to everyone.

Eventually things settled down and life went back to some semblance of normality. With no other information, Barry's death was put down to suicide caused by an overbearing guilt relating to his perversion.

Mrs. Barlow gave birth at a private clinic about 6 months later. Despite the premature delivery, the baby boy was healthy. Its ears were unusually large and its skin was slightly pinker than normal but The Barlows were ecstatic. To avoid any awkward questions they sold their house and moved to the highlands of Scotland where the heather was purple, land smelled of peat and people kept to themselves.

Mike gave up writing his novel. The controversy in the street had provided him with enough material to focus on a documentary about Barry the Paedophile. He finally got his best seller in the non-fiction category. He stayed in the street but stopped going out after dark. He also gave up smoking—the sound of the trees rustling no longer calmed him and he also moved bedrooms. He now slept at the front of the house even though it was a much smaller room. He claimed it was warmer there, being over the fireplace and that was the lie he clung to in the middle of the night.

Old Lady Jones's mind decided it had seen enough and flew out of the window never to return. The secrets of how and why she summoned the beast flew out of the window along with her mind. The authorities discovered her just before Christmas when neighbours became worried.

They discovered her huddled in an armchair in her front room. By the time they found her she was vastly obese and covered entirely in piles of egg wrappers that were also littering the house. She no longer spoke complete sentences. All she could mutter was something about the Easter Bunny being happy with his presents, which she repeated over and over. None of her teeth remained and her hands were caked in a brown matter that proved to be more than just chocolate. She died not long after in hospital.

When they discovered her lifeless body one winter morning they found the remains of one last chocolate egg clutched in her hands, sucked to the size of a seed. Winter replaced autumn, which succumbed to spring.

Frost gave way to soft rain as life slowly came back to the land. The trees started to sprout buds and fresh roots found the beast in its lair. As it awoke and smelled the fresh air it was happy. The season was right for it to be awake. The beast discovered that most of the trick or treaters had made their way to its lair. They huddled together in the darkness, quiet and subdued. The beast smiled. One by one it devoured them in silence but for a sickening crunching and slobbering. They didn't fight—they simply offered themselves up as sacrifice. After the broken hibernation it was exactly what the beast needed. The beast didn't eat Dave and Felicity though, who had made her way back through midnight streets to the lair. It looked at them with what could only be described as paternal love. It showed them the secret clearings, places where people still left gifts and sacrifices. The three of them spent the following months feasting on the gifts whilst watching the moon and counting the stars. Dave and Felicity held hands and they were happy, together at last.

As for Adrian, he had been getting gradually fatter since Halloween.

Around Easter time, Adrian felt his stomach cramp as he ate yet another chocolate egg. His parents dosed him up with cod liver oil and sent him to bed. The pain got steadily worse as he moaned and whimpered to himself. Eventually, with no other escape route, the thing inside him ate her way out. She looked down sadly at the dead father she would never know before jumping out the bedroom window. For a new born girl she was surprisingly agile. She sniffed the night air and her large ears twitched, picking up various sounds around her. Something or someone called out to her from a distance. It said to go north, where the flowers grew purple and the air smelled of earth. With no better plan in mind she set off, eventually to be united with her half-brother. But that, as they say, is another story.

05 Spells

It was Dad's turn to supervise the evening bath. His daughter Wendy was busy in the foamy water, mixing toothpaste, bubble bath and shampoo in a cup. Bemused at the intense focus given to this concoction, he asked,

'What are you doing?'

'Oh Daddy,' Wendy replied with the scorn only a 7-year old can muster,

'I'm making a potion from my spell book.'

Playing along, Dad asked, 'Will that make my hair grow back'? (his bald spot had been bothering him for some time).

'Nope, it'll turn you into a frog,' came the assured response. She continued stirring and muttering some 'magic' words. Getting into the spirit of things, when it was handed to him Dad took a small sip of her proffered cup. Pretending to drink, he swallowed a bit before spitting the rest out into the toilet when Wendy wasn't watching. As expected, the warm, minty yet bitter liquid was utterly vile.

With rapt attention, Wendy stared at her Dad but to her disappointment nothing happened. He didn't turn into a frog (and his hair didn't grow back). He was just her chubby, slightly balding Daddy, gagging into the toilet.

The next morning Wendy burst into the master bedroom, presumably to check whether or not Daddy was now a frog. Wendy didn't even try to hide her disappointment. She sulked at the bottom of the bed. All she could see was her sleepy Dad lying in bed. Teasing her gently, he laughed and scolded her for not making his hair grow back. Wendy stuck her tongue out in response. Dad followed suit, sticking his back.

She stared with interest at his tongue, but alas it was just a normal, boring, human tongue.

Scratching and stretching, Dad got out of bed and ambled to the toilet.

He daydreamed out the window as he relieved himself. A slight stinging down below made him make a mental note to drink more water.

Finishing off with a quick shake he looked down. The bowl was full of tadpoles.
His knees started to give way as he saw another tadpole squeeze out, wiggle free and plop into the bowl. He quickly sat down before he fell down. Wendy stood watching with a look of shock from the doorway.

She clutched the old crumbling spell book to her chest. She'd found it in the attic a few days back and had been fascinated with it ever since.

Snatching the book he frantically flicked through pages, barely taking in the odd pictures, vaguely Arabic script, and its strange smell of age and spice.

Wide-eyed and desperate, he flicked ever faster. He suddenly found himself believing in magic. He just needed a reversal spell. His stomach gurgled loudly. His innards started to writhe, followed by a spasm and a splash. The last thing he heard before everything went green was a deep 'ribbit' coming from underneath him.

06 King Bryan

Last night I died. Oh, don't look so scared now. It wasn't the first time. It's just one of the dangers of the job, I suppose. But it did get me thinking. I'm not going to be around forever, and I guess you're old enough to know the family secret. The truth is, we can alter time. Yeah, I know what you're thinking but I'm serious. You can't at the moment, but you will. Now, don't get too excited. It's not like we can travel through time. But we can change it.

We change time by making it go quicker or slower. When I slow time down, I can see and hear the things that usually move too fast for us.

I can see life squirming in a drop of water as it falls from the tap before exploding in the sink. When I speed up time, everything moves much faster. I can hear the trees chatting to each other. They don't say very much mind you. Mainly it's just gossip but they say it nicely and I can't help but eavesdrop.

It's this ability that lets us do our job. I can see 'things' the rest of the household can't see. Don't worry now. Most are harmless. Have you seen the old man who walks around the house at night, muttering to himself? He smells a bit funny but he keeps to himself. All he does is complain about how things aren't in the right place anymore. But there are other things, things that are dangerous. It's these that we need to watch out for. It's these that we need to protect the house from.

So anyway, where was I? Oh yeah, last night. Rain was falling softly, bringing with it the smell of the ocean. I was patrolling my territory, making sure all was safe and sound. Walking down the street my whiskers began twitching and sure enough, as I rounded the corner I was hit by a coppery smell so thick it almost knocked me over. I could see something crouching under a lamp post. The lamp post leaked rain, blurring things so I slowed down time and the shape came into focus. About the size of a small human, it was squat like a frog with long dangling arms and a large round head somewhere in its chest. The skin was blue but translucent, with red shapes twisting and writhing just under the surface. With the rain bouncing off it, it seemed to glow. The thing was hunched over something dead, pulling out splattering tubes of pinky red stuff. It turned to face me. The head had no eyes, no ears, and no nose—just a mouth. An impossibly large mouth filled with rows and rows of teeth. I swear it grinned at me as it stuffed pink tubes into its maw.

I slowed down time even more. This was different to anything I'd faced before. No way was I going to take any chances. I ran full pelt at the thing. Goddammit, but it was faster than me. We collided mid-air.

Despite the adrenalin surging through me, pain seared my body as a deep groove was gouged into my shoulder. I crumpled to the ground. I knew right then that I had lost a life. I'm not going to lie—I was scared and I screamed for help. I tried to stand up to face the thing again but my legs wouldn't stop wobbling. Blood dripped thickly from my shoulder in slow motion and the thing licked its lips, leering at me. It started to lower itself and I'm pretty sure I crapped myself in fear. It was then that I heard the other cats. From over walls and fences, around corners and under cars they came. Oh, it was a beautiful thing to see.

They flowed over the thing like a furry river, kicking and screaming, biting and scratching. Soon it was smothered and overpowered. Despite its struggles they held it down. The others parted, making a path for me.

I stumbled unsteadily forwards. As I got closer it grinned even wider, thick ropes of drool oozing down as it made a throaty chuckling noise.

With my good arm I slashed its throat wide open. Steaming goo spurted out of the gash and the thing began to shake violently. We all backed away from the juddering shape. With a sudden POP it disappeared, leaving behind the smell of excrement and a sticky puddle.

I limped away from the mess and turned to go home. The others bowed low showing me a respect I thought I must have lost. A few of the younger ones looked up as I hobbled past, eyes blinking their trust, before they quickly looked down again. I tried to walk as straight as possible.

Too damn full of pride, that's my problem. Trying to walk proud can hurt like a bastard let me tell you!

I eventually made it back home. Making my way painfully upstairs I dragged myself onto big brother's bed. He woke up, smiled sleepily at me and scratched my chin. Despite the pain, I couldn't help but enjoy the sensations flowing from his hand. I felt myself purring as the strokes sent waves of pleasure down my body. He fell back to sleep and I started licking my wounds. Bath done, I went to the bottom of the bed, curled my tail around me and settled down for the longest catnap ever. When I woke, he'd put down the good stuff in my bowl for me. Life isn't so bad eh?

And that, my boy, is how I died. No doubt you've heard the rumours that we've got nine lives? I don't know if it's true. I've not kept count of the amount of lives I've lost but I think last night was my eighth. If it's all true I might not be around much longer. When I'm gone, it's going to be up to you to look after the family. They need us to keep them safe.

But I'm not ready to go just yet. I intend hanging around for as long as possible. Okay, don't look so sad. I'm still here right? So how about you and me go on patrol tonight. What do you say? I'll introduce you to the trees and the moon. I'll show you my territory, my land. The land of King Bryan.

07 Stoned

The lure of the sea had always had a hold on Andrew. After the death of his parents he spent his inheritance on a camper van and a surf board and headed down to the Cornish coast to live the dream—a life of sun, sea and surf. For weeks he travelled up and down the coast, fuelled on coffee, homebrew and a seemingly endless supply of dope.

Every day he woke up whenever he wanted, surfed for as long as he wanted and smoked his way through the dream.

Alas the dream didn't involve a strong hygiene regime and the weeks of surfing every day, eating instant noodles and sleeping in a cramped, damp van played havoc on Andrew's skin. The sea, salt and sun made his baby soft skin dry and scabby. His once lush hair was now straggly and was slowly turning into thin blond dreadlocks. The scrapes and cuts from being bashed against rocks hidden under the surf failed to scab over and heal due to being continuously wet. If they did heal over they left his normally pink flesh scarred a dark grey colour, hard and scaly to the touch. The various tumbles under the foamy swell had caused him to lose a few teeth along the way so when he grinned he looked like an old shark leering at fresh meat. He had long lost contact with any friends from back home but if they saw him now they probably won't recognize him anymore.

Yet the lure of the sea was still too strong for him. Scabby skin, skanky hair and sore welts weren't going to stop him from surfing. When he was on his board, riding the waves, feeling the cold spray of briny sea he felt truly alive. When he wasn't on his board he could be found sitting on the shore, gazing at the ocean with a faraway look in his eyes.

He started travelling further afield in his quest for more surf. After exploring most of what Cornwall had to offer he headed north, ending up in the cold North East where surfers braved dark, Arctic waters set to a backdrop of abandoned industry. It was here that he got a text from his Uncle.

'It's your time. Come home,' it cryptically read. Puzzled as to what was his time, Andrew tried to picture his Uncle. He could only summon up a vague caricature of the man complete with bald head, bulging eyes, tiny ears, large nose and dry flaky skin. Just for fun he added a black cape to round off his caricature. He wondered if there was any more inheritance money on offer. After weighing up the alternatives of ignoring the text and surfing the wastelands of the North East or the chance of getting some more cash he started to pack the van up to make the trip back home.

Home was the Isle of Man, an island off the North West coast of England. Whilst many would say it was beautiful, to Andrew it was claustrophobically small and he had been glad to leave. The idea of going back there depressed him. However, the lure of potential money was motivation enough and so he set off to make the journey across the backbone of the country. From the other side of the country he could see about getting the ferry back home.

The start of the journey was uneventful. As his van puttered up to the crest of the A66 the sight of the Lake District opened up like a pop-up book in front of him. He parked the van in a lay-by to roll a joint and take in the view. As he'd been late in setting off the sun was setting and flooded the land with a soft warm light, bathing the countryside in golden rays. After the harsh North East coast it was a sight that warmed his heart.

Even the lack of ocean didn't stop him from soaking up the glowing vista. Too much natural beauty or maybe too much dope made him light headed and giddy. He didn't fancy driving in his current condition and so he was forced to spend the night in the lay-by, gently rocked to sleep by the juddering wagons that passed through the night.

He awoke the next morning to the sound of rain drumming on the roof of his van. After a quick cup of tea and a small thin morning joint he set off on his journey once again, pleasantly buzzed. Peering through squealing windscreen wipers, he navigated his van down the slick A66.

The splashing rain made him think of home and he began to daydream about what his Uncle might want. Since the death of his parents (missing, long since presumed dead) he had lost all contact with any of his friends and family back home. To get a text out of the blue from his Uncle was odd. In all honesty, to get a text at all from his Uncle was almost comical. Whilst he couldn't really remember his Uncle, Andrew was sure modern technology like texts would have been beyond him. A telegram would have been more appropriate. Lost in daydreams, he totally failed to take the turn off for Heysham and the ferry.

He felt panic surge up through his spine as he realized he'd missed the junction. Not having a map or GPS he only had a vague notion of the way to Heysham and passing Keswick only reiterated how lost he was. As he continued to drive his concentration and driving became more and more erratic as his brain tried to mentally calculate where he was. The desire to pull over and light up a calming joint was strong but he kept missing the lay-bys that whizzed by. Besides, the cars behind him were close—too close it seemed to his paranoid mind, still a tad fuzzy from his morning joint. He blindly turned off the road he was on and found himself on unknown and unmarked country lanes. As the roads narrowed the banks on either side got higher, hemming him in. His paranoia was now thrust into overdrive, and the insidious claustrophobia wasn't helping. With the rain still falling, obscuring the distant hills in low cloud banks, some of the smaller roads were transformed into little rivers and had been closed. He plunged down detour after detour at random in increasing desperation. Before he completely lost his mind he lunged out at what could only be described as a lifeline when he saw a sign that promised sanctuary. If not sanctuary then at least it sounded like a safe haven. And that was how he ended up at Whitehaven.

When Andrew finally arrived at Whitehaven he urgently sought out the beach to sooth his frayed nerves. His dry skin was itching like mad and all he could think about was how he wanted to get to the sea. No, he needed to get to the sea. This was no craving, it was a necessity. Almost through some animal instinct he found a section of beach and as soon as he set foot on it the stress drained out of him, making him feel weak with gratitude.

The beach he found was long and empty, stretching out into the distance before it disappeared into the sea. For the most part it was made up of bone white rocks and stones, bleached by years of sun, sea and salt. A bank of fog lazed over the sea and brought a scent of cold seaweed to the beach. Despite the lack of sunshine, despite the lack of surf and despite the lack of soft golden sand it was truly a haven to Andrew. To be so close to the ocean once more calmed his soul and he felt all previous tension oozing out of him. Peering into the fog he could make out a vague shape on the horizon which he guessed was the Isle of Man. Even though the thought of going home to that island depressed him, he still felt relaxed now he was next to his beloved sea. He would get to the ferry tomorrow or maybe the day after. His Uncle could surely wait a bit longer.

He sat on the stony beach looking out to sea. Through habit he had taken his board with him and it now lay discarded next to him as he sat, gazing out at the gently lapping waves. The bleached rocks rolled and shifted under his weight as he fixed himself an extra big joint to smoke.

As the drug hit his lungs the familiar blissed-out sensation spread out through his body. He smiled to himself as his soul soared free. Seagulls wheeled about in the air currents above and screeched obscenities at each other. The damp air felt good on his dry, hard skin and everything was right in the world once again.

He ended that day sat on the beach. It was just him and his joint, wrapped up in a warm hoody. The mist had lifted as the evening sun started to melt into the ocean. The dope combined with the hypnotic lapping of the waves started to work on him and he found his head lolling forward as his eyelids became heavier and heavier. Eventually he dozed off, never to wake again.

A few days later some locals walked down the beach searching for drift wood, maybe some cockles and mussels or anything else they could salvage. They came across Andrew's belongings. His bag, his surfboard and his towel were lying abandoned next to a large boulder. They looked around but the beach was deserted. Times were hard and that surfboard looked expensive. It didn't take them long to decide that the owner of the board and bag wasn't coming back. Quickly picking up what they could they scuttled away to sell the goods before anyone came out of the sea to claim them.

Days, weeks and then months passed. The large boulder sat forlorn on the beach in the morning mist. Andrew's belongings had long since been sold on and the rock was just another large rock on the beach. A few clumps of seaweed had anchored themselves to the rock along with some determined barnacles. As the morning sun rose to burn away the mist the rock started to warm up and a solitary gull came down to rest on its surface. By midday the rock was warm to the touch. It slowly started to wobble as a crack appeared down one side of the rock. The crack became a split which became a hole as a large, grey webbed fist punched its way out to freedom, startling the seagull into flight. Yes, the lure of the sea had always been very hard to resist.

08 Milk

By the time they had finished moving everything from the van to the house it was getting dark. Dave had hoped for a picture perfect moment, where they all stood arm in arm looking at their new house, complete with blue skies and glorious sunshine. As it was, his wife Emma was rattling around the kitchen trying to find the kettle while Lisa, his almost teenage daughter was stomping about upstairs, trying to pick a room. Still, the move had gone smoothly (bar a broken plate) and they had finally arrived.

Promotion had allowed Dave and his family the chance to relocate in the countryside. It was something they had talked about for ages and now with the extra money they could turn dream into reality. After several months house hunting they decided on a quaint village on the North Yorkshire Moors. It was big enough to have a shop, a few pubs, even a takeaway. Sure, the commute was far, but a commute over beautiful moorland was something Dave looked forward to.

It didn't take long for them to settle into the village. A couple of locals dropped by to say hello but other than that they were left alone. There was none of that 'you're not from around here' or goats head in the pub mentality his work mates joked about. One of the pubs even had its own craft beer. Lisa joined the local brownie group, which also included Girl Guides, Cubs and Boy Scouts. She soon made a few friends and even teased her Dad that there were some boys there. They were soon on first name terms with more than a dozen villagers. It would probably be fair to say that life was pretty much perfect.

Summer soon came around, and with it the long summer holidays. On his commute, Dave spotted a small petting farm type thing and on one particularly beautiful day with nothing better to do they decided to check it out.

The farm was set on open moorland, where the sky seemed bigger than in the city. Even if the farm turned out to be rubbish, the views would surely make up for it. As they ambled round, it soon became clear that the main attraction were goats. Lot and lots of goats. For Dave, the other main attraction was the almost all female staff. He noticed with increasing interest that they were all young and beautiful. Skin glowing with good health and fresh air, curvy figures barely hidden underneath work overalls. Dave snuck sneaky glances at the staff when he thought no-one was looking, getting him an elbow in the ribs from Emma once or twice. She had also noticed the female staff but to her the glowing cheeks seemed to be that of a woman in the first flush of pregnancy.

That made no sense, what with all the livestock around. She tried to put it out of her mind, annoyed with herself for getting broody. As for Lisa, she enjoyed the farm well enough. The baby goats were the prettiest she'd ever seen, with eyes that looked less alien than regular goats. They gathered around her, gently butting her for snacks and treats. Even though her hands stank of wool and butter, it was worth it. They really were supercute little goats.

Strolling around the farm Dave overheard two of the workers talking in German. It had been a long time since he'd practiced German but he wandered over and tried a few phrases. The workers stopped and stared, open mouthed. Then they started giggling and spoke back, in rapid fire German. Dave felt himself blush, completely lost as the language washed over him. The girls started whispering to each other, and it seemed to Dave their smiles turned to sneers. He made his excuses and shuffled off, wanting to go home all of a sudden.

On their way out they stopped by the small farm shop where they felt obliged to purchase some goats' cheese and a carton of goats' milk. The lady behind the counter made small talk and by her heavy accent it was clear English was her second language. Previous embarrassment still burning Dave's ears he muttered a subdued 'Danke' and luckily this time it was met with genuine warmth. He left the shop a new man and with an extra carton of goats' milk. Despite no-one really being a fan of either milk or cheese it had been a lovely day out. Making a few purchases felt like buying a souvenir of the day.

Back home, Emma made tea. They decided to try the goat milk. Even Lisa wanted to try a small glass. With the rest of the house silent, they gathered around the kitchen table. Dave made a great show of opening up a carton. Taking a tentative sniff, Dave made an over the top grimace, causing the other two to laugh. The truth wasn't far off—his stomach twisted at the heavy, oily smell. All three sipped cautiously at the thick, creamy liquid. Dave and Lisa couldn't bring themselves to finish their glasses but Emma slurped it down with relish. She licked her white moustache and then went on to empty the remaining glasses.

Over the summer months they paid a few more visits to the farm. Dave ogled the staff from a distance, Lisa petted the baby goats and Emma stocked up on more milk. With each visit they noticed the amount of visitors was increasing, and the farm expanded accordingly. Even their local shop in the village started stocking goats' milk, which suited Emma down to the ground.

By the end of summer Emma started to have a flushed face of her own as she discovered she was pregnant. It took them all by surprise. It certainly wasn't planned. But a trip to the chemist followed by the doctors confirmed that yes, they would soon be hearing the patter of tiny feet once again.

The following months passed quickly. Emma's rapidly expanding bump seemed to demand goats' milk and she chugged carton after carton. No cravings for lobster and watermelon, just goats' milk. Lynn at the shop joked that she reckoned Dave must have shares in the farm the amount of milk he bought.

Eventually the day of delivery came. The baby boy was born, big, and healthy, earning him the name Max and causing Emma a few stitches.

Max was also incredibly loud. From day one he cried, screamed, wailed, and cried some more. Dave began to look for excuses to be out of the house. A persistent smell of nappies and goats' milk filled the house. No matter how many windows he opened the stench was like greasepaint that coated the walls. However it was the constant crying that drove him up the wall. He couldn't remember when he last slept for more than two hours, and he stumbled around in a sleepless daze. Lisa seemed to cope better. She helped to clean the dishes, popped clothes in the washing machine and took herself off to school. Meanwhile, Emma tried desperately to get the boy to breastfeed. He latched on, suckled until she felt she was dry but then demanded more. They took to bulking up his feeds with formula. The only way to keep the wailing down was to keep him topped up with milk. So top him up they did, and enjoyed some peace.

The night of the great discovery Dave came home late. It had been a hellish day at the office, not helped by lack of sleep. The day had been spent floating from one meeting to the next, fuelled by coffee and Red Bull. Even before he opened the door he could hear Max screaming.

For the briefest moments he contemplated getting back in the car. As it was he opened the door, the sweet sour smell of baby shit smacked him in the face. He found Emma in the kitchen, trying to console the baby, purple and shiny through screaming. Through the screams Lisa managed to explain that the shop was out of formula. Dave sighed deep and heavy.

It looked like he was going to have to get back in the car anyway, and make the hour trip to the nearest town. He opened the fridge for yet another can of something sweet and sugary and saw the goats' milk.

The idea of leaving the house for an hour had its advantages but he was so tired he could barely think straight. He snatched a carton out of the fridge and poured it into a baby bottle. Giving it a quick blast in the microwave he tentatively tried the teat in the baby's mouth. To everyone's relief, Max hungrily slurped it down in one go. When the bottle was empty he burped and even smiled. For the first time since he was born Max slept through the night. The next morning everyone was awake bright and early, refreshed and full of optimism. No-one wanted to jinx it but it seemed like goats' milk was the magic key.

Sure enough, the combination of breast milk, formula and goats' milk continued to work. The baby slept and grew. It wasn't long before he was as big as his basket. Alas all good things have to end, and so did the supply of goats' milk not only in the house but also the village.

On cue, Max started to yell, his voice becoming raspy and ragged sounding. They tried regular milk, bouncing him, even some ambient music with whale sounds but nothing worked. The screaming continued, drilling directly into Dave's head via his throbbing ears. With a mixture of guilt and relief he got into the car to start the drive to the nearest town.

The road out passed the goat farm. It was late and the farm was surely closed, but Dave could see lights. Desperate hope sprang up in Dave's chest and he swung into the car park. As he got out of the car the gentle breeze of the moors felt clean and fresh. After the screaming house, the only sound now was that of blood rushing through his ears, as loud as the ocean. Feet crunching across gravel, he made his way towards the main building.

From their previous visits Dave knew where the farm shop was and that was his first destination. With no lights shining in the shop, he knew knocking on the door probably wouldn't do any good but still he tried.

After a few minutes of nothing but sore knuckles he decided to head towards where he had seen the lights. The farm was strangely silent.

No goats bleating or dogs barking. The breeze carried the scent of goat dung as he pulled up the collar of his jacket. He could see dim light from a large building that was never open during visiting times. In the darkness it was hard to make out the building other than its size, blotting out the stars behind. He tried the front door and, finding it open, walked in. Calling out, his voice echoed hollowly. Eyes slowly adjusting it looked like he was in a stable or barn. The floor was rough concrete and the place smelled of disinfectant and sour milk.

Inexplicably beds were lined near the walls in neat rows, made of black leather and shiny steel. Next to each bed was some form of apparatus.

Frowning, Dave moved to the nearest bed. The apparatus consisted of two pumps, making his mind lurch inside his head as he took in the significance of this. Yellow light escaped from under a door on the far wall so Dave headed in that direction. Without realising it he walked as quietly as possible across the floor, and with every step closer his heart picked up a notch.

Approaching the door, there was still no sign of anyone. He would have turned back but he needed that milk. He was also enjoying the fact that he would be hailed a hero, already going through the story he would tell Emma and Lisa when he got back home. His knock on the door reverberated loudly in the empty hall but there was no response. He tried the handle and the door opened. Instantly the smell of wet wool, rancid butter and dung stung his nostrils. His stomach surged upwards filling his mouth with bitter acid. Wiping drool with the back of his sleeve he took in the lone inhabitant of the room.

The goat was massive. As big as a horse, covered in glossy black hair.

The beast's hide was littered with scars and sigils burned into its flesh were no fur would ever grow. Rearing up on two legs the sex of the beast was clear and Dave fell backwards, horrified by the enormity of its member. Black and glistening, it was at least the size of his forearm. As Dave stumbled to get away the beast slumped to the ground, making a sad pitiful noise. The sadness in its voice made Dave stop in his tracks and look back. The thing had been tied down, thick ropes knotted around all four legs. The beast bowed its head, giving off a defeated air. On closer inspection, Dave could see how badly it had been treated.

Aside from the many scars, its thick hair was greasy and matted.

Where the ropes had tied the beast into submission, crusted blood and glistening welts circled its ankles. Seeing he was in no immediate danger, Dave looked around the room. Candles spluttered on various shelves, illuminating a single bed in the corner, stirrups on either side. He thought of that monstrous member again and shuddered.

The beast slowly raised its head and looked directly at Dave, making his heart skip a beat. It opened its mouth and made a noise that against all sanity sounded like words. Thick, guttural sounds dripped like cement from the beast. Dave stood, utterly confused. His overly caffeinated brain was already battered and skittered around the noises coming from the goat. Eventually the beast stopped and stood silent, looking at Dave.

He was at a loss. He wished he had never stopped at the farm, let along creep into this room. It wasn't until he saw what looked like tears in the beasts' eyes that he knew what to do. Warily, he edged towards the beast. Up close, the stench became stronger and he could see fleas move like grass in the wind on its flanks. Slowly, he dropped to his knees and started to loosen the knots that bound the creature. The beast remained motionless as he did so, and Dave didn't dare look up and make eye contact. Instead he focused on the task at hand. It was hard work—the ropes were thick, crusted with dried blood and other fluids but one-by-one each leg was released.

On freeing the last leg Dave stood up and moved back. The beast stood to face him. Panic lanced his guts. Shouldn't it move on four legs?

What next? Would the thing gouge him? Stomp him to the ground?

Something far, far worse? They stood facing each other for what seemed like an eternity. The goat slowly approached Dave, giving off not only a foul stench but also heat in equal measures. It put its forehead against Dave's and that was when Dave nearly lost his grasp on the world. Images flooded into his head, fast and vivid. First was a forest, trees impossibly huge and densely packed, mist swirling around the bases. There was the goat, on top of a mound, surrounded by bowing worshippers. The vision swiftly changed, showing trees being cut down and the forest thinned. The goat was still in its place, but the number of worshippers dwindled. Eventually, the beast was in some dark room with flames burning in the corners. Young women offered themselves in return for unknown favours. With that, the visions stopped and Dave was back in the room. His head spun, feeling like he had just got off a rollercoaster. The goat stepped back and dipped its head in what could only be described as a bow. With one last look at Dave the beast ran out of the door and into the night. Dave, realising he had been holding his breath, breathed out deep and slow, knees suddenly weak.

He drove home in silence, window wound down. When he finally arrived home it was late and the house was quiet. He peaked into the main bedroom and a grateful smile spread over him at the sight of his wife and son, both fast asleep and snoring. Stinking of goat, he crept to the bathroom. Standing under a scolding shower tears suddenly welled up and he quietly cried into the plug hole. He regained composure and dried both his eyes and body. Creeping into the bedroom, he contemplated kissing Max. In the end he didn't dare run the risk waking him, something he would regret for the rest of his life. Instead he slunk into bed, and lay staring at the ceiling waiting for sleep to take him as he listened to the beautiful sound of his wife and baby's deep breathing.

Morning sunlight drifted through the blinds, catching motes of dust lazily wandering around the room, waking the family up. Waking them all that is except Max. Max, who should have been crying for a feed, or chewing on a toy, was not in his cot. Emma screamed, collapsing on the floor. Dave, head still wrapped in sleep, raced around the house, searching every room. Lisa stumbled out of her room, rubbing her eyes awake. Max was no longer there. The back door had been smashed open. After another desperate search Dave had to face reality and call the police.

Eventually two harassed looking detectives arrived. They examined the door, commenting that it had been smashed from the inside out. Both made notes and asked questions that neither Dave nor Emma could answer. They both felt numb, shocked, and all they could do was drink tea. Over more tea the detectives let slip that there had been quite a few disappearances that morning. Just how many they couldn't say but their furrowed brows spoke more than the words that came out of their mouths.

The following days merged into one grey mass. Emma stayed in bed, hugging one of Max's toys. She simply couldn't take it in. Her beautiful baby boy, her Max—gone. It was just impossible for her to accept it.

How could someone have broken into their house and taken him whilst they were in the same room? It made no sense. She kept expecting him to be in his cot, waiting to be picked up and cuddled. Dave scoured the internet, trying desperately to find anything that might help. Like the police had said, Max was not the only one to go missing. Several other children were missing from the village, and the atmosphere was strange, subdued, like a thick mist had smothered the place. People greeted each other blankly, faces wax masks of incomprehension. In other villages similar abductions had also occurred but there was not one lead to follow. Life was turned upside down as the whole country joined in the mourning and the search. It wasn't long before the farm was searched and found empty. Its owners had simply disappeared, with no trace or clues to chase. The local papers posted some photos of the buildings, including the strange beds and pumps. Dave felt his stomach lurch at the memory of that night.

Alas no-one was ever found. The media got bored and found something else new. The country simply shrugged its shoulders and moved on to the next tragedy. Time did its usual trick of slowly healing wounds. Lisa and Dave managed to coax Emma out of her bed. Life would never be the same again but at least they had each other. When Dave suggested they put the cot in the garage Emma broke down and refused. He didn't ask again. It was several months later when he came back from work that he noticed Emma had moved the cot herself. Slowly but surely they pushed through the pain.

Several years passed. The family stumbled through life, barely coping.

Emma struggled to sleep at night, suffering from nightmares. Dave threw himself into work but also suffered from fits of depression. It was Lisa who brought the family back together. Being the youngest perhaps made her more resilient. She went back to Girl Guides and kept quiet whenever she had a bad dream. It was the second summer after Max had been stolen. Her Girl Guide troop had decided to go on a midnight hike. It took some persuading but eventually she was allowed to go.

The moon was full and flooded the moorland in pale white light. As they tramped across soft heather they fell into little huddles to chat and gossip. The moor stretched out for miles, as the moon hung low to the ground. Up front there was a bit of a commotion and soon all the girls were clustered together. On the horizon they could see something the size of a horse, but running on two legs. Even at a distance they could see the massive horns curling on either side of its head. As they stared, the thing was already running away from them, closely followed by other shapes. It was hard to make out what they were, but Lisa knew.

She knew that one of those running things was Max. Tears silently flowed down her cheeks, cold in the night air, as she saw her baby brother one last time.

She made her excuses and ran all the way home. The house was dark and silent as she let herself in. Bounding up the stairs to her parents bedroom her heart pounded. Shaking them awake, she launched into what she had seen. Dave sat on the bed, red-eyed and bleary. Emma stared at something unseen. Lisa wasn't even sure they were listening but she blurted out everything she had seen regardless. When she had finally finished, she fell silent, panting and slightly dizzy. Neither said anything for a moment. Chest heaving, Lisa sat gripping the edge of their bed, willing one of them to say something. Finally Emma reached over and hugged Lisa tight, rocking her as she cried saying over and over how she knew, she just knew Max was still alive. Moments later Dave put his arms around them both and all three cried and cried. The three of them stayed huddled like that for some time. Lisa slept in their bed that night. For the first time in a long time they all slept a deep peaceful sleep.

09 Spider Chords

The band practised in a dank and mouldy studio downtown.

It was run down and skanky but they could play as loud as they wanted without complaint.

To get them in the mood, they usually scored some weed from a tall thin Egyptian man called The Pharaoh. Tonight he asked if they fancied something a bit more…decadent? It was cheaper than the usual and so there they were—hash smoked, heads mashed and ready to rock.

The bass player began by slapping a basic groove, complete with closed eyes and sloppy grin. The drummer listened for the heart of the beat and joined in with a rumbling pattern. The guitarist waited to get into the mood, strumming a few minor chords.

Downstairs in an alley the Pharaoh listened, grimacing at the mundane rock music.
The guitarist frowned, shook his head and switched ideas. Fingers arched like spiders, he started thwacking out new, discordant noises from his guitar that screeched with raw energy.

The Pharaoh's grimace twisted into a grin. Better.

From the deep, dark void of space movement began. Monstrous shapes in the blackness found flutes made from the bones of titans, picked up drums skinned with lesser gods and began playing. Spheres of colour oozed and pulsated, throbbing to the hideous rhythm. Slowly, the Blind Idiot God stirred from its ancient slumber and began squirming in the middle of the swelling cacophony.

Back in the studio, things were cranking up. Sweat saturated the air, moist and dense. The guitarist was practically attacking his guitar and stomped his pedals like they were cockroaches.

Outside, the Pharaoh stared upwards, watching the clouds build and gather in the night sky obscuring stars and hiding the moon.

Cats hissed at the dark, dogs cowered in puddles of piss. Children hid under blankets, lovers huddled together. Young mothers dreamed of strangling their babies, the elderly contemplated drinking that bottle of bleach under the sink.

The Daemon Sultan was swelling, waking.

The Pharaoh started to snicker as the storm gathered.

Inside the studio, the bass player was in a trance. The drummer sweated, pale and glistening, drumsticks blurring. The guitarist was building a tsunami of noise, getting closer to a shattering crescendo. Closer, ever closer……TWANG!

Several strings snapped followed by a FUCK of pain as the guitarist sliced his index finger open.

The drummer stopped bludgeoning his kit and the bass player slowly refocussed. The only sound was the warm hum of amps and the panting of the drummer. The tension was broken when the bass player shouted 'I got to pee!' and ran out of the room.

The others laughed and began packing up.

Deep in space, bone flutes and skin drums were thrown away and the swirling chaos gave way to emptiness once more. Clouds disappeared and stars twinkled in the now clear sky.

The Pharaoh sneered in disgust and slunk off into the night. Oh well. There was always another day, another band.

10 Nine Lives

So I guess you've heard a rumour about how we have nine lives right? Well, they are not exactly rumours. But I'm also guessing they are not quite what you think. It doesn't mean that we have nine lucky escapes, or nine near-death experiences. It means we actually die nine times. How do I know? Easy. I'm on my ninth life. I can remember each one of the nine, in all their painful glory.

So the next question is what happens after the ninth? Your guess is as good as mine. All I know is that after going through nine, I'm tired.

Maybe this is it, this is the last life and there's no more after that. Truth be told, I would be okay with that. My nine lives haven't all been easy, so a nice rest? Yeah, that would be okay. But I'm jumping ahead of myself. Let me explain a bit and maybe then you'll see.

My first life was okay I guess. There were five of us and I was the smallest, always the last. I used to follow the others around and on the whole it was okay. Sure, I got the last scraps of food, the chewed up toys, but I got them. I survived. Our owners looked after us well enough. But I was small and I was slow. On my last day I was hit by a car coming too fast round the corner. It was over quickly. I didn't even realize what had happened. One second I was crossing the road, the next? Well, the next was the beginning of life number two.

At first it was confusing. I was a cat but not the same cat. But that's what was so confusing. I was a different cat, but I could remember everything from before. Now I was bigger, stronger. I wasn't last anymore. After my first life, I was determined not to follow. I was going to lead. For a while, all was good. The others followed me. I would decide where we were going and the rest would follow me. But one-by-one my brothers and sisters disappeared. I'm not sure where they went.

Eventually it was just me. I missed them so much it hurt. My adopted family looked after me well but the loss of my real family was too much and I guess my heart broke. My bones started to ache, my teeth hurt and eventually I just wanted to close my eyes and forget it all. One day I went to sleep and when I woke up, everything started all over again.

Life number three wasn't so great. It took me less time to understand what had happened. Soon I was up and running. I had experienced two lives. I knew what I wanted to do. I wanted to be alone, and not have a broken heart. I prowled the streets at night. I started to realize that I was in the same place as my other two lives. For one thing, the air had the same salty tang to it. I discovered a place where there were fresh eggs and I took to sneaking in at night to steal one or two. It was there that I found I wasn't the only one who stole eggs. The fox took one look at me, decided I was competition and in a snap life number four began.

I got angry. Why was this happening to me? Why did it just go on and on, pain after pain? Nothing made me happy. I hissed at others, beat up those smaller than me and hurled myself at those bigger. Eventually I was taken to a cold, echoing place. It stank so much it hurt my nose. I could hear others crying, hidden away. I didn't like it there and I got even angrier.

I was soon moved to another place that was much, much worse. I was put in a small room that was cold and draughty. People came to look at me and I hissed defiance at them. It wasn't long after that I was taken to one final place. White and still, the room reverberated with strange noises. The last thing I felt was a sharp prick at the back of my neck.

When it inevitably started all over again I was less angry, less frustrated.
I guess I had gotten all that anger out of my system last time round. I started to think a bit about what was going on and even the why of it

all. By now I was convinced I was coming back to the same place every time. Like I said before, it smelled the same every time. But it was more than that. I started to recognize places, remember the smells of the fields, the sounds of the streets. I spent most of my fifth life in deep thought.

My adopted family was quiet and peaceful. They made no demands on my time and I spent many an hour thinking whilst watched dust motes float through the air. I passed gently from fifth to sixth. After all that soul searching, life six was a bit more active. I prowled the same old streets, talking to any cat willing to chat. I met Bryan, the self-proclaimed king of the neighbourhood. He was old, grumpy and slept long hours but would chat to me from time to time when the mood suited him. It was he who explained about the nine lives. He was on his ninth and had found a kind of grouchy peace with the world. Eventually things came to their natural conclusion and six became seven.

Life seven was when I started to understand the why of it all, albeit through a confusing start. My new family was small—only two of them. I was young but quickly established a comfortable routine. In the evening I would make sure the house was safe for the night before curling up on the female to enjoy a gentle stroke or tickle. On one such evening I was enjoying a little attention when I had to jump off, hair standing on end. I could hear a strange noise from inside her. As I crept back to listen again

I realized it was a different heartbeat, coming from below her normal beat. It took me a moment or two before I understood she had another inside her. The new beat was different, faster and more insistent.

When two became three I was suspicious of this new thing in the family.

Everything about it was different—its smell, its sound, even its shape.

And yet I found myself drawn to this little creature. It was pure and innocent and I found myself being more and more attached to it. We would spend more and more time together. It grew into a she and she became everything to me. I would sleep on her bed, she would feed me, I would wait for her to come back from wherever she went, and she would groom me like my real mum.

I can still remember the day when I truly started to get that clarity, that understanding I'd been searching for. She came home, crying. I didn't understand why. She lay on her bed, sobbing great heaves of tears, gulping air like a fish. Confused, I climbed on top of her and started to purr. It's all I could think to do. And that's when it happened. Her tears dried up. The pain inside her melted away. It was a revelation. I knew about purring. I had used it many times before, mainly to heal myself.

But I never knew it could heal others. From then on, I paid special attention. It didn't take long to understand the power I had inside me, a power I had been too selfish, too busy to even notice before.

When I moved from seven to eight I was devastated at first. I had only just discovered this power of mine and I knew she needed me. We had connected in a way I had never experienced before. My new family were kind, and I had a new brother who kept me laughing with his playfulness. But I never forgot her from my seventh, and even the antics of my brother couldn't keep the sadness away.
I didn't know it at the time but soon everything was about to turn itself on its head. As per usual, I was feeling sad, and so had decided to go for a little walk by myself. Eighth time round, I knew the area pretty well so no chance to get lost. But as I rounded a corner I saw myself. My heart skipped a beat. I didn't look like I did during my eighth life, but it was me. I couldn't tell you which

version of me it was, but it was me. Before I could say anything my earlier self was off over a wall and gone, leaving me standing there with my head spun around in so many directions.

As I wandered home it slowly dawned on me. Not only was I in the same place every life, I was in the same time. As this sank in, I knew I couldn't stay home anymore. Saying goodbye to my brother was hard.

We bumped noses and nuzzled each other one last time before I left.

But I just had to go and find her. I took to the streets and it wasn't long before I found my previous family. My little flap was still there just like it always was but I hesitated. Would they know it was me? I pushed my way in and crept into the front room. They were still three but slightly older. She was there, looking down at me with a puzzled expression. She bent down and rubbed my ears in the exact spot I had always loved. I was home, back where I belonged.

The rest of my eight passed in what I can only describe as heaven. To be back home with her was just beyond everything and anything. But she was older, and she was around less and less. I didn't mind. She still came home, and when she did she still stroked me and fussed over me.

Near my end she came home with her own little one and I knew she was going to be okay without me. I had given them my love, my power I had experienced how I was able to purr away their pains and ease their hearts. I was ready for my final life. And so here I am, my ninth life.

My last family are old. They love me and I love them. In the evenings, I settle down on either one and as they stroke me I purr. I can feel my purring sending healing waves into their aching bones, easing the pains they both suffer. At night they lay side by side and I snuggle myself down at the bottom of the bed. From time to time I shuffle myself up onto either one of their chests and listen to the gentle ticking within. I feel her pain more than his, and I lie next to her for longer and longer.

My purring calms and relaxes her but alas life moves on.

Now it is just him and I. As night settles I lay on top of his chest. His ticking has changed; it doesn't feel the same any more. It misses a beat every now and then and I think he is close to passing over.

I suspect tonight is the last night. Slowly and painfully I manage to get onto the bed. My bones are old and delicate and it takes me longer each time. As I settle next to him he reaches over and strokes my ears one last time. I purr, but I can't prevent his ticking from stopping. I knew his heart had broken when she had passed and now, finally, it has had enough and stops.

As I lay here in the quiet of the night, I know this is my last life. I slow my breathing, calm my nerves and close my eyes one last time.

Or so I thought.

When my eyes open things are different, very different. I see Bryan who smiles at me. There are others in the shadows and while I can't really see them I sense their presence. We chat and joke about past lives.

Bryan explains that I have two choices. I can be free at last, and enjoy an eternity of happiness and comfort. Or I can go back and start over, with all the pain and suffering there is. I sit and think for a moment. I think back over all the hard times I've had, and there were many. But then I start to think about the good times, the friends and family I've had, the love I've given and received. It doesn't take me long to decide.

And so, I open my eyes. I see my new brothers and sisters. I see my new family. They reach into our basket with nothing but love in their eyes.

I see one young girl sitting alone and I wobble over to her. At first she doesn't know what to do as I crawl into her lap. I settle myself down and she tentatively strokes my ears and chin. As I start to purr I can feel her love pour over me and I know I've made the right choice.

11 Snake Charmer

As I stepped off the plane the heat smothered me like a thick oily blanket. I knew it was going to be hot but this was something else. As I trudged through turgid air to the terminal, tarmac sucking my feet, sweat instantly poured off me. So this was India.

It all began a few weeks back. My brother had been murdered whilst in Delhi. Even now as I write this, it still hasn't sunk in. The last time I saw him he was tanned, healthy and getting ready for his next adventure.

Now he was dead, his remains in an Indian mortuary waiting for me.

Our parents had long since passed away and I was pretty much the only family Mark had. I explained to my wife what had happened and she helped me pack for the trip. Passport and visas in place, I was off.

My first real taste of India was the taxi from the airport. As I got in I had to fight the urge to sneeze, the smell of incense as thick as pollen.

I gave the driver the name of the hotel. He nodded and off we went.

On his dashboard was a little plastic Elephant God complete with bobble head and incense coming out of his bum. The traffic was insane as I gripped my bags with knuckle white hands. The urge to jump out, dash back to the airport and get the next flight home was strong. Cars swarmed like flies around a dead carcass, following no discernible traffic law. People ambled across the road, oblivious to the honking traffic. We stopped and another man got into the passenger seat. He exchanged a few words with the driver before turning to me.

'Hello my friend,' he grinned, 'first time to India?'

'Erm, yes, first time,' I muttered.

My stomach lurched and not just from the traffic. My hand tightened even harder on my bag. I'd done my homework, read my Lonely Planet guidebook. I knew all about a wide range of scams. Sure enough, he informed me that my hotel had closed down but as luck would have it he knew a much better one. I thrust a piece of paper at him, muttering something about confirmed booking via email. He didn't even read the paper, just went back to chatting with his mate. He jumped out soon after. I allowed myself a small smirk of satisfaction. Maybe India wasn't going to be so hard.

My taxi driver pulled up at what looked like a back alley in a slum.

He pointed down the alley at something, presumably the hotel. Blinking in the sun, I got out of the taxi. He put his hand out of the window. I smiled and shook it, thinking we'd somehow connected in that short journey. He jerked his hand back in disgust and sped off, shouting angrily. It looked like India was going to be bloody hard work after all.

I stood still, looking around. What the hell was I doing? Mark was the traveller, not me. The street was bedlam. Kids chased each other, leaping over leaking trash. Men stood in small groups drinking from small dirty glasses. There was even a cow, munching on a cardboard box as its tail flicked at the swarm of flies. I took a deep breath, and instantly regretted it. A ripe sweet-sour stench filled my lungs making me cough. Trying not to look lost, I strode off in the direction the driver had pointed. Within about 3 minutes I stood outside the hotel, lathered in sweat. With a mixture of relief and triumph I entered the hotel and walked up to the front desk. A man with humongous eyebrows and matching moustache glared at me. As I explained who I was, his shoulders slumped and a broad grin spread across his face. He launched into a tale of woe about the loss of business he had suffered since the murder, talking quicker than I could follow. He shook his head sadly, all the while assuring me his hotel was the safest in Delhi. Eventually conversation dried up and he handed me my keys. Moments later I was safely deposited in my room. I had arrived.

The room was clean, white with a single bed and desk. As I opened a window I was greeted with a swell of noises, smells and thick bars.

Definitely safe if not quiet. After a shower and a snooze I could no longer put off what I was there for. Mark's body was in the Police Station. His belongings had been delivered to my room and now I sat looking at a small pile of clothes, books, laptop and sponge bag. As I began rifling through his stuff sadness flooded over me. These were, after all, the belongings of my only brother, murdered in this hotel. I swallowed, throat thick. This was no time to get sentimental, I had to be strong. His old laptop sat on the desk, covered in faded stickers. I tried switching it on but the battery was dead so I put it on to charge. With nothing else to do I ordered room service and called it a night.

The next day began slowly. Last nights' meal sat heavy and now my stomach creaked and groaned. The laptop had fully charged but was somewhat predictably password protected. After trying a few random things my heart leapt when it logged on. I allowed myself a little sad laugh. The password was the name of our family dog from almost 10 years ago. I paused. I felt like I was spying on my dead brother. But I wondered if there was anything on the laptop that might indicate what had happened. The Indian Police had been very evasive about any investigations. What lay before me hidden inside that laptop?

The desktop picture showed a recent photo of Mark smiling proudly between Mum and Dad. It was taken a few years back when he had been home for a while. Mum and Dad had passed away almost one after the other. We had chatted that their love for each other was so strong they couldn't be without each other. Not for the first time I had to choke back tears. Mark had his usual cheeky grin as he squinted in the sun, his blue eyes looking even bluer than usual. A dark suntan made his hair seem almost white. I opened up Explorer and started having a rummage through the contents of the laptop. I didn't really know what I was doing. Maybe I was simply putting off going to identify his body.

Before I knew it, several hours had passed. Despite just sitting there, I was coated in a greasy film of sweat. With my stomach complaining, I had a quick shower and went to get something to eat.

Leaving the safety of the hotel I looked around at the street. The chaos of yesterday hadn't subsided. The guide book recommended a café that was within a couple of minutes walk from the hotel and so that's where I headed. I found it quick enough and darted in, eager to be away from the crowds. Inside the heat was kept bearable by large ceiling fans, churning round and round. Music trickled out of a small tinny speaker and I squeezed myself into a corner table. Seconds later a young man handed me a crumpled laminated menu. Ordering a banana pancake and tea he disappeared, leaving me to take in my surroundings.

Travellers lounged about in white linen clothing or baggy pants, all looking tanned and comfortable. I sat there, sweating through my shorts onto the plastic chair and felt even more out of place than ever. Food came quickly and I wasted no time in eating. It was only when I stopped did I realise just how hungry I was. I left some money on the table and snuck out before anyone said anything.

Back in the hotel, stomach nicely full, I went back to the laptop. We'd kept in touch with Facebook before he disappeared. I still preferred to think of it as disappearing rather than being murdered. I knew I was kidding myself, but by doing so it allowed me to cope. As I scanned through a few random documents I found what appeared to be a diary of sorts. The feeling of prying into someone else's life came back to me and I hesitated. However, I had come this far. Maybe there was something in there that the police had missed, something that would shed light on this mystery. Scanning through, it became obvious Mark was interested in snakes.

I knew he liked animals, but I was taken aback by this revelation. Had we drifted so far apart I didn't even know my own brother? As I read on, I found this interest in snakes was actually more sinister. It seemed Mark was interested in holy men and shamans around India, but only those connected with snakes. He wrote about his search for genuine snake charmers. Not just circus acts (although he encountered plenty of those) but people who could charm snakes into doing all kinds of impossible things. He had heard of a charmer who could make snakes stand upright, so rigid they appeared to be like wooden staffs. For the most part he was often disappointed but somewhere along the lines he stumbled across something he referred to as Yig. I googled it but found nothing. As I read on, Yig became his main focus. What Yig was, he didn't explain.

I finally reached the last entry—made a few days before he was murdered. Despite the heat I felt a cold shiver. My eyes burned from poring over the laptop screen but I simply had to read on. He wrote about how he had been approached by two men who claimed they could take him to meet some dude called Sufi John. As I was reading it I could picture Mark going along with them—so like him, and so unlike me.

Sufi John turned out to be blind, fat and very high-pitched. Mark didn't go into great detail but the bloke didn't even have eyes, just two empty sockets. Mark seemed to believe he was something called hijra. When I googled this word I got more luck than searching for Yig. Hijra meant something like eunuch, which would explain the high pitched voice. You live and learn. I continued reading. Sufi John performed a magic show for Mark. From what I could gather it was pretty standard until the climax. I had to read the next bit twice, just to make sure that was what Mark had wrote. He described how a snake was summoned, and then plunged through one of Sufi John's eye sockets, exiting seconds later through the other. An illusion but one that Mark obviously enjoyed. He had been driven back to the hotel, and that was pretty much it. Three days later they found his dead body.

I sat back and looked up at the fan. As it whirred above me I tried to picture Mark sat in this hotel, writing about that night. Questions buzzed around my head like wasps. What had he seen? What was this Yig thing he kept mentioning and was it connected to his murder? Who was Sufi John? Did he have anything to do with the murder or with Yig?

My back ached from being hunched over the laptop so I got up, hearing pops and cracks as I stretched the pain out. I showered one last time, moved the bed directly under the fan and tried to sleep.

Heat, noise and the whine of an invisible mosquito all conspired to give me the worst night's sleep. I eventually gave up, showered night sweat off, and ventured to my favourite café for breakfast. I ate slowly, trying to put off the inevitable—identifying the body. I had planned on walking to the morgue but decided against it. It was only about 8am and the sun was already up, turning the pavements into mud. With vendors already setting out their stalls, the streets were already crowded making me feel claustrophobic. I went back to the hotel and asked for a taxi. Another Ganesh lounged on the dashboard—this time a static version with fake flowers. The taxi fought its way valiantly through the traffic. Everywhere I looked I saw people—huddled in tight groups, squatting by the road or loafing around. They all seemed to be staring at me so I focused my attention on Ganesh. I was glad to arrive at the police station.

Once inside I stated my business to a bored looking receptionist who pointed me to a large cluttered room. Full of overflowing cupboards and old wooden furniture, I perched on an old rickety chair. I didn't have long to wait before I was escorted to the morgue and the body of Mark. The harsh chemical smell of the room made my nose burn and stomach churn as much as the dead body in front of me. I struggled to focus as my stomach flipped and somersaulted. As my head swam I was asked to identify that it was indeed my brother. Somewhere in the middle of this nightmare I noticed the eyes. Or rather, the lack of eyes.

The doctor cheerfully told me that both had been cleanly scooped out and was almost certainly the cause of death. As he pulled back the lids to show me I lost the battle and vomited violently into a sink.

Dignity in tatters, I signed the release forms. I headed back to my hotel room. Another taxi, another dashboard God. This time it was a plastic figurine of Hanuman, the Monkey God. We drove in silence.

Despite everything, or maybe because of everything, I slept better that night. I had done what I needed to do. Now I just had to wait a day or two before it was time to fly back home. I decided a trip to the zoo might be interesting. Maybe it was a family thing, or maybe it was the last connection I had with Mark but I was curious about snakes. I wanted to visit the zoo and see if they had any snakes. It turned out to be a big mistake. The zoo was a grim collection of putrid cells, smelly and depressing. I headed back to my hotel in a funk. The relentless noise, swarms of people and endless assault of stenches was starting to get to me.

As I walked up to my hotel I felt myself tense as two men detached themselves from a wall. As I slowed down they smiled through thick oiled moustaches.

'You look for Sufi John, no?' Said the nearest and I tensed even further.

How did they know I had been reading about Sufi John? I hadn't spoken to anyone about it. We exchanged some polite chit-chat and eventually I felt myself calm down. Despite feeling nervous, I agreed to meet Sufi John. I wondered if there might be some information about my brother I was missing. Now more than ever, I missed him. Any connection to him was worth a risk and so off we went. I was ushered into a large private car and we set off. There was no bobble-headed Ganesh or Monkey God in this car. Instead an ugly humanoid snake sat glaring at me, doing nothing for my nerves. I tried not to look at it as the car made its way to some unknown destination. The streets got wider and quieter as the houses got bigger. This was a different, richer side of India. We eventually pulled into a large drive, lined with tall spot-lit trees.

I was led into a large house. Everyone took their shoes off and I followed suit wincing slightly at the sweaty foot prints I left behind me. The men headed off down a corridor and I followed suit, heart pounding.

We entered a large, murky room. The fan on the ceiling span so slowly it barely shifted the air and I felt damp with sweat. Incense was burning in every corner, but there was another smell underneath that I couldn't quite place. Cushions littered the floor and I was gestured to sit.

After a short wait a small fat man wearing dark glasses entered. He was dressed in a white linen robe and he introduced himself as Sufi John in a high-pitched voice, with only a faint hint of an accent. We made small talk and I felt myself relaxing. He was small, fat and appeared totally harmless as he giggled at everything I said.

I mentioned my brother Mark but Sufi John just gave a shrug and a curious head shake. He clicked his fingers and gave me a smile. Baskets were brought into the room. Thin piping music swarmed out of nowhere and snakes began slithering out of the baskets. I found myself moving closer to the wall. The source of that other smell became clear—it was the earthy, animal smell of snakes. A smell that to this day I can still recall. They slithered over Sufi John slowly and sinuously. Each snake had a diamond Bindi on its flat head, presumably glued in place. Sufi John made various hand gestures and the snakes stood to attention, or flopped to the ground, all in unison. I had to admit, it was pretty impressive. It wasn't long before the show moved on to the grand finale.

I expected Sufi John to take off his glasses. I thought I was prepared.

I wasn't. Sufi John de-robed to reveal his glistening nakedness. I couldn't help but stare at his emasculation. I'm not a doctor. All I can say is it looked tidy. Instead of his manhood, he was left with a small plastic pipe and an empty sack. He unscrewed the pipe, revealing a dark hole. Without thinking I took out my camera and flashed off a couple of shots before an attendant appeared from nowhere, signalling no photos.

As I pocketed my camera a small silver snake rose out of a basket that had been placed in front of Sufi John. It reared up to face his waist before promptly plunging into the hole, making me wince. It disappeared into the empty sack, only to reappear moments later. As it did so I realised I had been holding my breath the entire time. Snake safely back in its basket I clapped heartily more out of relief than anything else. Sufi John dressed and we shook hands. I asked how much for the show. He smiled almost coyly, shook his head and left. I never saw him again.

The drive home was in silence. I pondered over what I had seen. Sufi John was clearly an entertainer. A very extreme one, but still just a showman. The driver held out his hand as we arrived at my hotel. I'd learnt my lesson and I pressed some slightly damp notes into his open palm, noticing the faded snake tattoo on his wrist as I did so.

I was too wired to sleep so I treated myself to a few beers at the small restaurant. Four or so beers later I weaved my way back to my room, pleasantly drunk. The beer had helped to relax my nerves. I figured I'd done everything I needed to do in India. I'd identified the body and signed the release forms. The episode with Sufi John was unexpected but I was glad I had gone. It seemed an apt way to say goodbye to Mark.

I was satisfied I'd done enough to call it a day and head home. I told myself that enough times I almost believed it. I got into bed and settled down to sleep.

I was woken from a dream about bagpipes. As I surfaced from sleep I sluggishly wondered why I could still hear piping. The street lights outside filled the room with vague orange shadows. Something slithered up my leg and all sluggishness disappeared. Wide awake I looked down to see a thin snake hissing towards me. Rather, hissing towards my boxer shorts. I lay there watching it, unable to move. Sure enough, it was homing in on my nether regions. Instinct took over and in a move that surprised myself I kicked the snake off the bed with a scream. It hissed angrily and rose up. I hurled the bed sheet over it, and as it thrashed to clear itself I picked up my shoe and threw it hard. Someone or something must have been smiling down on me as my shoe connected soundly with the head of the snake. It collapsed but I took no chances, pounding the head over and over through the sheet until it went red with blood. Eventually all movement stopped. I stood, sweating and panting, shoe in hand as I recovered my breath. I switched on the light and slowly removed the sheet. Shoe still in hand, I peered at the snake. A knock on the door almost caused me to soil myself. The manager was outside, asking if everything was okay. I let him in, keeping my eye on the bloody mess. Together we examined the snake. Despite being mashed up, I could just about make out a small diamond glued onto its forehead.

It wasn't long till the police arrived. I mentioned Sufi John but with nothing else to go on the conversation went nowhere. The police suggested that as snakes could easily be bought at various markets in Delhi, it could be anyone. They promised to make some enquiries, making it clear that I should leave it alone. After what seemed like a lifetime they left. I slumped exhaustedly onto my chair. Enough was enough. I just wanted to go home. And yet as I sat there, waiting for the sun, my adrenalin addled brain refused to rest, bouncing questions around my head, like so many rubber balls.

I powered up the laptop and uploaded the few photos I had quickly snapped from the show. In the gloom of the room I could just about make out Sufi John. A few tweaks, a bit of magnification, and his face was clearly visible. On one photo his glasses had slipped down. My brother's eyes stared straight at me. My heart skipped. Despite the heat I shivered as the sweat froze to my skin.

Once the idea had started to grow was no uprooting it. It made no sense but at 4am in the morning anything is possible. Had Sufi John somehow stolen Mark's eyes, and used them as his own? Had he sent a snake to steal another set of balls he needed? To steal those balls from me? A snake couldn't unlock doors but it could slither between bars through an open window.

I ran to the window and closed it with a bang. After double-checking it was shuttered, I made sure the door was locked and cranked the fan up as high as it would go. I sat awake until the sun had risen. Enough was enough, and I certainly wasn't going to wait any longer than I had to.

The taxi to the airport had no Snake God on the dashboard. The driver had no snake tattoos. I felt as safe as I could under the circumstances.

We headed towards the airport. Traffic was as insane as ever and I slumped down on my seat. As I did so, I caught sight of the driver in his rear-view mirror. His necklace had a snake on it. He smiled, a cruel thin smile.

I wasn't going to take any chances. I grabbed my bag and jumping out of the taxi, straight into honking traffic. Unable to leave his car, the driver shouted impotently at me, waving a fist. Heart pounding, I jumped into the next auto-rickshaw that trundled by. With just a plain, everyday Elephant God, we made it to the airport with no more upsets.

The rest of the homeward journey was uneventful. Despite the hum of the engine and several in-flight beers, I couldn't relax. As I sat and watched movie after movie, I kept looking around me, unable to rest.

After an eternity the plane touched down in England and I got back to my apartment with no further ado.

I'd like to say things settled down once I was back in England. For a time, everything was normal. I went back to work, but never stayed out for long. It wasn't long that I began to notice them. Men wearing matching linen robes. Men with flashing necklaces. Sometimes I'd catch a glimpse out of the corner of my eye of a flash of white. Sometimes I would see a gentleman sitting in a corner of a restaurant, pretending to casually read a paper. I started getting random phone calls to my office.

Somehow they must have got my address. I would see men standing underneath the street lamp staring up at my apartment. I had wild fantasies about going outside and confronting them. But I'm not a brave man. In the end I just packed my bags and left.
I now live in the far north of Scotland, working in a cannery factory.

It's boring, stinks of fish, pays badly but is safe. I spend the evenings drinking beer whilst scouring the internet for any information on India, snakes, or murderous cults. If you look hard enough you can start to see connections: a snake missing from a zoo; people dead from mysterious bites; bodies misplaced from hospitals and so on. I keep my doors locked and my windows shut even in the middle of summer. A few nights back I woke to the sound of pipes. There was nothing outside, just the trees gently swaying in the breeze. Just a dream. Have you ever noticed that the rustle of leaves sounds a bit like the hiss of a snake?

12 These Guys

[Marcus]

Right, everything is ready to go. Weather forecast looks good—a clear night and a full moon. Can't ask for more than that. Dave said his Dad is going to get him some beers, which is also good. No beer, no party.

What's this text from Paul? Hmm, just going to take a shower first and then he'll make his way down here. Okay. Just need to get some more firewood, and then wait for everyone else to arrive. This is going to be the best beach party ever! At least 12 people have said they are coming on the Facebook page so that means there'll be at least 15 of us. Throw in some beers, some girls, what could go wrong?!

[Paul]

Fuck this day. I swear if Marcus texts me one more time I'm going to lamp him. It's just a party on the beach. If that wasn't bad enough, Mum asked if I was out Trick of Treating tonight. I mean, seriously, why even think to ask if I'm going trick or treating. I'm friggin' 17, I haven't been trick or treating for ages. Anyway, I'd best get ready. Quick shower, maybe crack one off. Dave said he's probably going to have to bring his sister along and she's pretty hot. Might need to keep the wolf from the door. Who knows, this party might turn out to be okay after all.

[Dave]
Beer, check. Cool shirt, check. Fresh breath, check. I think I'm ready to go. Just got to wait for Angie to get ready. Why I've got to take her I don't know. She did say the twins were coming as well though so hey, who am I to complain! I wonder if I could get it on with both of them at the same time. Would that be weird? Dunno, but I'd be happy to find out! Oh, shit, there's Marcus again. What's taking Angie so long?

[Marcus]

Where are they? I've text them both about a million times. Oh wait, there's a reply from Dave. Cool. He's on his way. With beer. And his sister. Oh Jesus, she's cute. Damn it, I've been lugging all this wood around. I probably stink. Shit. Okay, it's cool. Breathe. Okay, better.

A few beers and I'll be good. I'm funny after a few beers, everyone says so. Right. Let me get this fire started, get the mood right. It's getting a bit chilly down here on the beach. Looks like there are a few other parties going on. Pah, ours will be the best one for sure.

[Paul]

Jesus, are you shitting me? How many texts? I've only been in the shower like 10 minutes. There must be about 20 texts from him. I'd better get going before he has a heart attack or something. Oh cool, Dave has got a case of beer from his Dad. Nice one dude! He IS bringing his sister. Hmm, better slap on some aftershave just in case.

She's pretty cute after all. A little splash down below as well. Who knows what the night will bring?!

[Dave]
Finally she's ready. Those twins are hot. Walking behind them was a good choice. They both keep looking back and giggling. Hope they're not laughing at me. I've got the beer, my arm is looking buff keeping the case upright. I reckon I look pretty cool. This could be a great party.

The skies are clear, a nice breeze, a few stars are out already. Yeah, man, this is going to be great.

[Marcus]
Ahh, there's Dave. And his sister. Whoa, she's looking good. Oh dear lord, the twins as well. Oh fuck. Gonna be hard to choose between the three if I have to. I need a beer. Relax, dude, you've got this. You've organised the party. This is your time. Count to 10. Be cool.

[Paul]
Oh here we go. Yes, I can see you, Marcus. Stop waving your arms, you look like you're trying to flag down an aeroplane or something. At least Dave is here. And yes indeed, there's his sister. Hmm, and the twins.

This party might not suck after all. And some beers as well, good man Dave! Right, quick breath test and we're going in!

[Dave]
Okay! It's all starting to kick off! Marcus did a cracking job of the fire, the moon looks awesome, we've got beer and girls. Let's get it on!

Marcus finally looks happy. As long as he doesn't get drunk, we should be good. He can be a right idiot when he's had a few. Right, let me have a beer and see if I can get something going on with the twins. Game on!

[Marcus]

Finally, everyone is here. Paul smells like a tarts purse, did he bloody swim in aftershave?! I guess he needs all the help he can get, the ugly get. He better keep away from Angie, I'm definitely in there. She's already flashed me a smile or two, I'm sure. Oh, that beer is good. I can feel a buzz already. No one else has turned up yet, but it's early. Not much of a signal down here but I'm sure more will turn up later. Shit, I've finished that beer. Another one won't hurt eh?

[Paul]

Fuck me, calm it down Marcus! If he keeps it up, he'll be puking before long. Still, more chicks and beer for me. Angie seems to like him for some reason. Whatever. There are two twins, let me see if anything happens there. Looks like it's just us so far. Wonder if anyone else will turn up?

[Dave]

Come on Paul, give me a break! Can't you see this is the dream? Twins, man, twins! At least he's leaving my sis alone. The way Marcus was going on, I thought this was going to be the party of the century. All good. I can see a few dudes coming now. Hope they've brought their own beer, like. My Dad only brought us so many, and Marcus has already chugged a few.

[Marcus]

Ah ha! More people! Only three of them but it's a start. Man, they are big. Whoa, is that dude naked?! No fucking way! Don't stare, don't look. Jesus, that's a big cock. Have they just been swimming? They're dripping wet. The sea must be freezing this time of night. Don't stare…damn, I just stared at his knob again. Oh good, they've sat down near the fire. Shit. They look older than us. I don't recognise them from college. Not very chatty, but that's cool. At least their junk is hidden away. Cool, Dave has offered them a beer. Looks like the other two have some clothes on. They must be drunk, but that's cool. This party is finally taking off…

[Paul]
What the hell? Who are these losers? No way. Is he…yes, he is…surely not…I can't believe it! That guy is fucking bare-ass naked. That's not right. I know it's the beach, but get some clothes on. Man, he's buff.

Look at those muscles. Hmm, is that a bit gay? Jesus, they stink. Smells like they have been wrapped in seaweed or something. Oh do not sit next to me. Okay, sit next to me, that's just great. Have a beer, yeah, that's cool. Just don't try anything. Please. I hope they don't start a fight.

Still, look on the bright side. With the twins being so frigid tonight, I might get a sympathy snog if I get my arse kicked.

[Dave]
I don't know these three. They look serious. From University? Maybe it's a prank or something. I mean, who walks up to a party naked?

I just can't believe he's naked. I mean, I'd be cool walking around naked if I was that muscly but still. He's naked! Okay, he's sat down near me. Should I offer them a beer? I'll offer them a beer. That's a cool thing to do. The other bloke looks like he's got a bottle of wine or something. Where's my sister? Okay, cool, Marcus is with her. He looks a bit freaked out but he's close by. Not too close. That's good. I like him, but she could do so much better than him. Okay, this guy likes beer. He even smiled at me. Relax, Dave lad, just three people enjoying Halloween. Nothing to worry about. Even if one is naked.

[Marcus]
These men are pretty okay. Not kicked up a fuss or anything. They don't say much but seem happy and relaxed. Oh man, what? You want me to drink that wine? Seriously? That bottle looks like it's got seaweed on it.

Shit. Everyone is watching me. Better have a sip at least. Man up. I can handle a bit of wine.

[Paul]
Hahahah! Yeah, Marcus, you just cough and splutter! What a wuss.
Here, let me show you how it's done. Time for ol' Paul to show you how a man drinks. Down the hatch!

[Dave]
Steady on there Paul, looks like he just drank half that bottle! Still, at least he's not gagging like Marcus did. What a fanny. Oh cock. My turn. Balls. The twins are both looking. Paul seems alright with it. Ooh, that smells nasty. What kind of wine is that? Right, here goes.

[Marcus]
Fuck me that was…

[Paul]
…probably the worst…

[Dave]
…thing I've ever drank.

[Marcus]
Whoa…

[Paul]
…what the…

[Dave]
…hell?

[The Family]
Welcome, brothers, welcome to The Family. You are now one with us.
All is one. All thought is one. All life is one. You are the shepherds. Go forth. Bring the flock to us. Our time draws near. Go. .

[Later That Night]
Safe to say, the rest of the party went a bit strange. The three friends reeled in confusion. Marcus vomited, splattering the sand with hot beery puke. The other two experienced the vomiting. They experienced the acidic burning sensation in their

noses and the retching afterwards as keenly as if they had vomited themselves. Marcus started muttering about maybe he'd drank too much wine, or beer, or both. Paul told him to stop whining, told himself to stop whining up. Dave looked down to see his sister flirting with him, and felt his gorge raising again. Or was it Marcus? Three over-worked brains shut down as one and they all passed out. The girls sat for a while, chatting to themselves. They couldn't believe the three boys were such light-weights. No-one had drank that much beer, but all three of the lads were flat out cold. Dave's sister kicked him in the ribs, trying to wake him. All three of them groaned as one, causing the girls to giggle. They tried again, and again all three boys groaned in unison. They quickly tired of the game, sighed, shook their heads and went in search of another party further down the beach. Dave's sister wasn't too worried. He was a big lad, he could look after himself. He just couldn't handle his beer. As they left they noticed only one of the new arrivals was left. The handsome one with clothes on.

He smiled, nodding at them, and they giggled as they strode out into the night.

The three woke up in the early hours of the morning. A damp mist had risen up, seeping into their clothes and bones, stiffening their joints like old men. The fire had all but gone out, smouldering away in the morning mist. As they stood up to stretch out the pain the realisation that last night was real. Whether they liked it or not, they were now a whole lot closer. They were intrinsically connected. As they looked around, that disjointed sense of confusion continued. It was at some point during this swirling nightmare that they (as one) realised the Family was still with them, watching them patiently. As he watched them, they watched themselves through him. Slowly he explained what had happened, how they were now connected with not only each other, but with all The Family. As he droned the information into their brain, he also explained how they could control what was happening, and try to disconnect themselves from each other, to try and have a semblance of normality. They practiced and slowly their panic lifted, along with the mist. The sun rose, shedding light if not heat.

With some effort they were able to stagger off to their respective homes to sleep off their hangovers.

The next morning began with difficulty. Dave woke up, needing to go to the bathroom. Only he tried to go to where the bathroom was in Pauls' house, not his. Before he knew what he was doing, he found himself pissing into his cupboard over his socks. That wasn't too bad. Poor Marcus woke up to a fountain of urine arching towards the ceiling.

Panic swirled up, and all three struggled to remain calm. They chatted without speaking and with an effort managed to practise the techniques they had been given. Slowly the panic settled itself down to sleep and they began to get things together.

Even when things started to even out, the call of the sea pulled each of them. It called to them endlessly. Whilst not loud, the call was insistent, insidiously lapping against them like the very waves of the ocean. If they listened carefully they could hear others behind the call, The Family.

It wasn't all bad. In fact, it wasn't long before things became very good.
College became easier. With the three of them working together, their grades started increasing. They started acing subjects each other was good at. With this improvement in college came confidence. With this confidence came an attraction from others. Both students and teachers, male and female, started to be drawn to them. It wasn't long before the three were hot items around college. Something they didn't fail to notice—and take advantage of.

[One Year Later]
Over the coming year, the three reached to full maturity, the dominant alpha males of the college,

leaders of the pack. Life treated them well, turning them from slightly awkward, spindly youths into tall, athletic and muscular young men. They excelled in all water sports, winning college swim meet after swim meet. Their sexual drive and attractiveness increased exponentially. By the time the year was over, more than two thirds of the college had been seduced by either one, two or all three of the trio.

On Halloween night, all those impregnated by the three felt a calling from the sea. Before they knew what was happening, they flocked to the sea, gathering together on the beach. A full moon rose, yellow and swollen as it dripped into the ocean. The night was cool, rumours of winter in the air. The crowd stripped off, standing hand in hand at the water's edge.

No-one spoke a word. Walking slowly out, they didn't stop until they were up to their armpits in the freezing waters. Despite goosebumps large enough to rival the craters on the moon, no one shivered. They stood in lines up and down the beach, waiting.

When the moon had severed itself from the sea and was riding high in the sky, everyone convulsed as one, sending the eggs incubating inside them into the sea. Strings and strings of eggs voided into the frothing waters, turning it into a thick soup. On cue, all The Family came forth, leering and erect, and finished the impregnation.

[Two Years Later]
Not all eggs survived. Many were eaten by their own kind, others by more natural sea creatures. But a good portion did survive. And grow.

And grow some more. In the year that followed, they came back home, hopping and flopping over the shores of that town. Not all were fully formed, covered in barnacles and seaweed, but some were splendid specimens of gleaming muscle. Regardless of shape or form, they ravished, raped or loved the town, depending on your point of view.

The town didn't put up a fight. It simply rolled over like an obedient dog, whimpering as it pissed itself.

As for our three boys, they had long since disappeared from the world, languishing deep in the ocean. They no longer remembered their previous life. Family, parties, beer—all things of the past. Now they were one with the sea. As it ebbed and flowed with the moon, so did they. The time was coming when the sea would reclaim the land, and they would be ready and waiting.

13 The Path out of Ulthar

I first visited Ulthar many years ago. In my youth I had spent much time reading of its rich and venerable history. I guess I had become somewhat obsessed with the place, and so to finally be there was a dream come true. It was everything I had imagined.

Quiet cobbled alleyways, swept clean every morning, spiralled out at seemingly random patterns from the bustling city centre. All around the city ranged sheer cliffs that nearly joined together to form a protective circle. One cliff, higher than the others, pointed skyward like a finger.

The locals named it Lovers End after a tragic suicide pact that took place many moons past.

As per legend, the city was filled with cats. Everywhere in that fair city I saw them. They lounged away the daytime heat, stretched out under dappled shade. As the evening cooled the city down they would saunter at leisure, free and proud. The history books tell us that the cats in Ulthar have attained a status close to holiness. People leave out bowls of food and water and the cats are treated with reverence and respect.

On that first visit I spent the weeks ambling down leafy avenues and eating in shaded cafés, always surrounded by cats. They would curl their tails around my legs as I sat munching on flat bread and savouring the local sweet wine. I fed them small titbits as they purred happily on my lap.

It was the last day of my trip that I met her.

I was just finishing my meal with a cup of thick gritty coffee when she jumped up onto the table. With a coat of soft white hair and eyes of blue and green I was transfixed by this most elegant of cats. I tried feeding her my scraps but she gave me a look that could only be described as disdain. The waiter smiled indulgently at the cat and informed me that

'Princess' would only eat the most expensive fish on the menu. Amused but suspecting some tourist trap I ordered the fish and treated myself to a final glass of wine. The waiter presented it with great flourish, even going so far as to have put the fish onto a small silver platter. Sure enough, Princess ate with great delicacy. Satisfied she looked me square in the eye, blinked slowly and bowed her petite head. She hopped down from the table and sauntered away.

I walked home slower than usual, enjoying the balmy evening of what I thought was to be my last night in Ulthar. I was aware that I was swaying slightly, and I grinned as that last glass of wine spread through my system. The night sky was studded with stars as a full moon rose lazily over the cliffs. It seemed to me that there were even more cats than usual. More and more appeared, hopping onto walls and climbing down from trees.

Soon I was surrounded but oddly they remained silent.

No mewing for snacks or affection, no hissing at rivals, just the quiet pad of paws on cobbled streets. Maybe it was that last wine, a loose cobble, or an untied shoelace. Whatever it was I tripped and fell flat on my face. Winded, I lay on the ground groaning. I rolled over, only to find myself on top of a blanket of cats. They took off at once rushing through the city. The speed was immense; the wind blew past as we raced onwards and upwards blurring the stars above. After a moment or two I realized we were heading out of the city and up towards Lovers End. My mind swirled and all I could do was lay there as we sped closer and closer to the peak.

As we reached the summit my stomach was filled with ice as I saw we weren't going to stop. The cats were surely going to jump off the cliff, sending us all to a certain death. Frantically I tried to move, to get off, but it felt like I was drowning in a sea of fur. The edge was rapidly approaching and my heart almost stopped as we bounded ever closer.

Seconds before my imminent death Princess appeared on a rock and gave a loud meow. The cats instantly halted with not so much as a skid.

For a moment I kept still, breathing hard. With no more movement I attempted to stand. My legs shook with fear as I tried to walk away from the edge.

Princess sat on the rock, looking down at me. The cats started mewing restlessly behind me. Princess nodded and they instantly began jumping off the cliff. I cried out in horror as they flung themselves into the night sky. Unable to look away my horror turned to amazement as one by one they changed into so many tiny stars floating up towards the moon.

Mesmerised I watched as the stars ebbed and flowed. Eventually the last cat jumped and gracefully rose upwards. I stayed on Lovers End for some time, struggling to comprehend what I'd just witnessed. As the night cooled I walked home slowly, deep in thought.

That first trip was the start of many journeys to Ulthar. I took my wife on our honeymoon; I took our children on countless trips who in turn took their children. The years have fluttered past, weathered with happiness and adventures. Now I'm old and my dear wife has long since passed. I've lived to see my children grow up to be kind and strong, a family to be proud of. I've seen them grow their own beautiful families.

I have no regrets.

As I write this, I'm sitting on the balcony of my hotel in beloved Ulthar.

I know this is my last trip here. Despite coming back many times previous I've never experienced what I saw that first visit, those cats floating away like dandelion seeds up to the moon. And yet the city is still as full of cats as ever before. On every trip we are visited by a beautiful white cat with blue and green eyes, just like Princess.

Restaurants have come and gone over the years, but they all seem to know Princess and what I can only assume are her offspring. It quickly became a family tradition to buy them their expensive fish dish. I would watch with a smile as they finished off their meal before giving me a bow and a slow blink.

I see Princess every day now. A part of me has started to believe she is the same cat I saw on that first trip. As crazy as that sounds I'm almost certain it is her. She comes to visit me as I sit on my balcony, enjoying the warm evening air. After rubbing her ears around my legs she curls up and purrs contentedly on my lap as I stroke her soft velvety ears.

Tonight is my last night. As I look down below the cats are gathering under the street lamp, moths dancing around the soft light. They sit expectantly, patiently waiting. Princess arrives and sits on the balcony watching me. She looks keenly at me as if to ask if I'm sure. I smile and nod. My time has come. I want to take that path out of Ulthar.

I am ready.

14 Destination R'lyeh

Colin loved his new car. Shiny, clean, packed full of gadgets, it was every boys dream. It had automatic lights, automatic wipers, multi-environmental A/C, satnav—you name it, it had it. Even though it was costing him a small fortune it was worth it.

He sat in the driving seat, playing with the satnav while he waited for Rachel to get ready. To pass the time he punched in 'humorous' place names to see if the satnav would pick it up. So far, it had found the hamlet of Twatt (12 hours distance), Fanny Avenue (2 hours away) and Old Sodom Lane (5 hours away). For fun he typed in R'lyeh, expecting nothing. His heart skipped a beat when the machine announced it was calculating the route to R'lyeh (only 37 minutes away).

His inner geek fist pumped the air—this was just too cool to miss. When Rachel got in the car he pleaded to go. She sighed but agreed as long as they could to her Mum afterwards. Agreeing to the visit and anything else, Colin took off at speed. He could picture the kudos he would get from having his photo taken next to a sign post saying R'lyeh!

35 minutes later, they were bouncing down a country lane. It had been an uneventful journey, but the satnav assured they were almost there.

There were no houses nearby and there had been no signposts for that all important selfie opportunity. Instead, they drove down a snake of a road that the satnav promised would take them to R'lyeh.

Too late, Rachel screamed at Colin to stop. The car flew into open space as the road ended, leaving only the North Sea and a few surprised gulls squawking at them.

As the car crashed into the water, their screams doubled as cold salty water flooded in. The wipers kicked in, optimistically naïve. The headlights cut two beams of light through murky waters. As Colin fought to keep his nerves in control he switched off the wipers. A morbid curiosity made him leave the lights on.

From out of the depths came the creatures. The headlights illuminated too much of what they were. Sickly white under the halogen glare from the car, like dead fish, they appeared misshapen and fleshy. Some were humanoid in shape, others clearly not. A few were clothed in scraps of rotting rags flapping in the current, most were naked but for seaweed and barnacles. They swarmed and writhed around the car. The flooding water stopped, only to be replaced by the stench of rotting fish.

Disgusting as it was, the air was breathable.

Rachel and Colin sat holding hands, wide-eyed with shock. The car creaked and groaned under the pressure as the creatures bore the car forwards. Slowly a dim green light became visible in the distance. They both jumped when the satnav beeped. The last thing either of them heard was 'You have reached your destination'.

15 Circus of Crows

First came the crows. Everyone in the town noticed them. For one, they flew in formation, like an arrow. For another, they had leaflets in their beaks which they gave out to the delighted crowd. We laughed at those beautiful birds, with their shiny black feathers and yellow beady eyes. They hopped on our hands and let themselves be stroked, twitching under our eager fingers. On the horizon a dust cloud gathered, and we knew the circus was coming before it reached our town.

The circus arriving was big news back then. Our town of Rolla, Missouri was much smaller than it is now, and circuses didn't pass through very often. Oh, we got our fair share of travellers. Good ol' Route 66 was always good for people passing by. But a circus? No, that was something special. The town practically buzzed with excitement.

We watched from a distance as big, hairy men heaved and sweated to erect the main tent. The old folk muttered about having to lock their doors, what with all those carnie folk and all, but us young 'uns couldn't wait.

I was just 16 at the time, never been in love and never been kissed. The summer of love was just a hint of incense in the air, a rumour carried on the breeze, and The Beatles had long since invaded. When the crows arrived, it was the middle of summer. The days were long, hot and sun-baked, and the nights short, warm and sticky. I lived with my elderly Grandma, Mamma and Poppa having passed several years before. We had our little wooden house on the edge of the farm, surrounded by fields of corn. Despite her age, Grandma was a shrewd business woman and rented out what was our farm to the neighbours. They did the work, and we got a healthy share of the profits. Grandma always insisted on a small potato patch in memory of Grandpa, and she planted small flowers around its edge, a memorial to her one and only love. The two of us spent many a long evening on the porch during that summer, sipping sweet chilled lemonade as the crickets chirped a nightly serenade.

The night finally came when the circus was open. The whole town had been talking about it for days, tension building like a storm, and I think everyone was going to go. I dressed in my finest outfit, excitement bulging inside me, straining to go. Grandma pressed a dollar bill into my hand, holding me as she did.

'Now you run along and have fun, you hear?' Her normally sing-song voice hard and strong. 'But be careful out there. It's a strange old world, stranger than you might ever know.'

'Oh Grandma, don't be silly,' but the seed was planted in my head, a seed which immediately began to grow with every step into town.

I met with my friends and the three of us headed out along with the rest of the town. I remember it like it was yesterday. The sun was slowly going down. A silken golden evening, pollen dancing in the air, with a gentle breeze bringing just a hint of relief. We paid our entrance fee and entered the circus. It was like a who's who of the town. Everyone was there. People strolled around in their Sunday best, tipping their hats to each other and chatting freely. The air smelled of hot dogs, sweat and cotton candy. We three clutched ourselves and pretended to ignore the local boys.

After ambling around for some time, it was time to head to the main tent. The acts were supposed to start soon and I remember wanting to get a good seat up front. It wasn't often the circus came to town and I wanted to make the most of it. We were pretty lucky, not right at the front, but with a great view. The buzz inside the tent was electric.

People laughed with each other, and it felt good to be alive on such a night. Straw had been thrown down on the ground, and the air was heavy with the fresh horsey smell of it, mixing with perfume, sharp sweat and popcorn. We perched on hard wooden benches and giggled at what was to come.

We didn't have long to wait. The lights flicked off, hushing the crowd instantly. We sat there, huddled together in darkness. With a bang, and a few screams and laughs, a bright spot light lit up the centre of the stage. There stood the most handsome man I think I had ever seen. He was tall, with steely blue eyes that prowled around the audience. I don't remember what he said, but I remember his accent. Rich, European, exotic. I think I fell in love right there and then.

What followed next was a staggering parade of acts. First up came a woman, skin as dark as Grandma's morning coffee, hair curled and oiled. She was beautiful, but the snake she had coiled around her shoulders terrified us girls. We shrieked as she caressed the thing, smiling at it with slightly parted lips. The snake in turn wiggled its forked tongue back at her and the men in the audience whooped before being slapped by their wives.

Next up came an elderly Chinese magician, with three golden birds bobbing and weaving in line behind him. From a town where men worked the land with large shovel-like hands, it was strange to see a man with such long fingernails. We watched with open eyes as he performed trick after trick, his birds keeping their beady eyes on him.

The climax of his show was when he transformed the birds one-by-one into small, slender, exotic women, dressed in red silky dresses. I envied their sleek lines as they danced around him, their faces white with red lips. I looked down at my own cotton dress, shapeless and frumpy, and scolded myself for being so graceless.

Luckily, a comedy act followed, taking my mind off my ugliness. Small dogs, wearing dresses and hats, frolicked around the centre and we howled with laughter. They all looked so serious in their little outfits, we couldn't help but clutch each other to stop ourselves falling.

They left, replaced by a huge hairy man and his bear. They wrestled, they danced, they span round and round until they became a blur. I was quickly confused who was who until they stopped, hugged and bowed in perfect unison.

The crowd bellowed their appreciation before settling down again. The tent became quiet. A misshapen man, old and withered like an ancient apple tree, shuffled on stage. He had with him a mangy looking monkey on a thin rope. He walked with a slow, shuffling gait, as though every step caused him pain. Eventually he made it centre stage and looked around at the crowd. He pulled out a battered guitar, and after a quick tune up started playing. The crowd remained silent as he somehow coaxed beauty out of his broken instrument and voice. I forget the words, but it was a song about how he missed his dead child, how he longed to be with her, to hold her one last time. When he finished, noses were blown and sniffs could be heard. Mrs. Cranston from the bakery had her head on her husbands' shoulder and I remembered she had lost her child not so long ago. My throat felt thick and my friends had also fallen silent. The strange looking man bowed and the crowd erupted into thunderous applause. He didn't smile, but nodded his acknowledgement.

The scabby monkey dashed around with a tin cup and the sound of coin on tin could be heard for many a minute.

The mood changed once again as the ringmaster came back for the finale of the night. He had with him a lion, a massive beast, bigger than anything I ever could have imagined. The crowd oohed and ahhed as the two of them strolled around the stage, perfectly at ease. The ringmaster looked around the audience and his eyes fell on me. My heart bounced into my mouth, and my stomach burst with a thousand butterflies. I looked down at my feet, cheeks burning. Had I imagined it? I dared look up again. He was still staring at me and my stomach shot forth another burst. He smiled then, and my knees buckled oh so slightly.

I don't really remember the rest of the show. I seem to recall him putting his head in the mouth of that huge lion and the crowd clapped with wild abandon to see such a thing. Before I knew it, the show was over. When the clapping and cheering had died down, people started to file outside, and we floating along with the sea of people. The mood was high, but all I could think of was the ringmaster's eyes as they found mine. I replayed those scant moments again and again, enjoying the strange crunching feeling in my stomach. We milled around for a while as the crowds slowly departed. Eventually, we drifted away and started to make our own way home. I waved goodbye to my friends, and headed down Jones Street. Darkness had fallen, throwing a warm blanket of stars over the sky. My heart was still pounding and before I knew what I was doing I had double backed to the circus. I wanted to find the ring master, wanted to see him again. For the first time in my life I felt alive, rash and giddy. The fields of corn spread out before me, and I knew he would be waiting for me.

The circus was still awake when I got back. Most of the crowd had gone, but there were still a few stragglers. No-one questioned me, and with stomach churning and heart pumping, I darted around the various tents. It was crazy, I knew that, but now that I was back, I couldn't stop.

From time to time, I had to duck into dark shadows to avoid laughing crowds of people as they made their way home. But nothing was going to stop me. I knew I was right, I knew what I had seen and felt in my heart.

It didn't take long to find him. I could hear the lion making a sound not quite a growl but more like a purr. A purr from the biggest cat you could ever imagine. As I got closer, I could see light flickering in a large caravan with a faded picture of a lion painted on it. This had to be where he stayed. I crept closer now, doubt starting to work its way into my confidence. The caravan creaked from some movement within and I froze, half expecting the door to fling open and my hero calling me to him. The door remained closed, unfathomable, and I inched forward to the caravan.

A yellow light spilled out from the small windows and I managed to hoist myself up to peer through a grubby pane. My heart all but exploded to see the ringmaster, my ringmaster, standing with his back to me. He was naked, and I could see his muscled back, perfectly formed. I felt something other than my heart and stomach. I felt that sacred valley between my legs open up, ready for this glorious creature.

Not for the first time that night, my knees weakened and I almost lost my grip, causing me to momentarily lose sight of my future love. When I recovered, what I saw threw my mind into a maelstrom. The ringmaster was still there, still naked, but on an unmade bed lay the lion. It was on its stomach, looking back at the ringmaster as he worked his meat into the beast. I watched, unable to look away, as he thrust himself back and forth, the lion arching its back in what I could only imagine to be throes of passion.

My head span as an explosion of disgust and confusion made me lose my balance. I ran off into the darkness, not caring where I went, tears blurring my vision. There was no-one left in the circus now and I just wanted to be home, wrapped in the comfort of my own bed. Before I knew it, I was hopelessly lost. Panic started to well up, making the stars above spin in ever decreasing circles. I whirled around and lurched in random directions.

I ran, faster and faster, until my lungs burned so much I thought I would collapse. Why was I still in the circus? It hadn't seemed that big before.

I stopped to catch my breath but as I did so I became aware of a group of men ahead of me. They were laughing and chatting and I stopped still, hoping to be invisible. I started to turn around before they noticed me but I was too slow.

'Hey there pretty girly, what are you doing out so late?' came a voice from the group. Despite my panicked state, I recognised the accent.

The gentle lilt, almost sing song nature of the voice was like my Grandmas, which could mean only one thing. They were Irish, or at least of Irish descent.

I stopped turning. They were all walking towards me. In the darkness, their features were shadowed, and my panic started to raise once again.

Instinct took over and I turned and ran, tripping over a tent rope as I did. Hitting the ground hard, I saw stars. The group of men surrounded me. I'd read all about young girls in circuses. Was I to be abducted?

Sold into slavery? Raped? I wanted to be sick. As they jostled around me, I couldn't bring myself to look up so I focused on their boots. Dirty, workmen-like things, worn and dusty.

'Are you alright, Missy?' said one of them. The voice was soft and tender.

A ripple of concern spread amongst them. This was not the sound of a group of rapists, or so I told myself. I took courage and looked up, straight into four worried faces. It was still hard to make out details in the dark, but I could see their kind expressions and I felt my fear start to drain away.

'You gave us a bit of a turn there, no word of a lie,' said another and all at once they began babbling. I felt myself smile at how foolish I had been. They did most of the talking and I just listened. Their voices sounded so musical, it was like they were singing to each other rather than talking.

'I think I....well, I'm not sure....but,' I stammered, not sure how to explain what I'd seen.

'What's that now?' said one of the men.

'Well, it looked like I saw the ringmaster,' I managed to get out, confidence growing, 'and he was, erm, with the lion.'

'Oh he was, was he?' said another, laughter in his voice.

'Come with us, let's see what this is all about, eh?' and with that they all moved as one, me stuck in the middle. Herded like cattle, I had no choice but to go with them. Sparks of panic started to flare up again.

The men continued chatting, exchanging glances at each other. In an impossibly short space of time, we were back in front of the caravan with the faded lion. How was that even possible? I had been lost for ages.

One of the men strode up to the door and knocked. There was a short pause before the door was flung open. And there he was, no longer naked but topless. Despite what I had seen, he was still so handsome.

'What is it? Do you know what time it is?' he said and then his blue eyes fell on me. My cheeks felt so hot, I was sure they glowed in the dark.

'So, did you enjoy the show?' he asked, and for a moment I wondered which show he was talking about. I didn't have to answer. A woman appeared behind him, olive skinned and so perfectly beautiful I think I hated her. But there was no sight or sign of a lion. I frowned. I could hear the men behind me chuckling softly, making my cheeks flush even more.

'Come back tomorrow, young lady. On the house,' and with that he went back inside, shutting the door, dismissing us like school children.

The guys talked indistinctly amongst themselves as we wandered back.

They led me to the circus gate and then insisted on taking me home.

The moon was high and bright, lighting up the roads. The breeze made the traffic lights sway gently but at that time of night, there were no cars on the road, and the lights talked to themselves. Here and there, a crow stood on a fence post, watching us.

Safely home, I fell asleep as soon as my head hit the pillow. Wrapped in the thick feathers of a dream, I woke late, sun shining onto my pillow.

After my chores were done, I went back to the circus. The air was dry, dust rising with every step on the path. The circus seemed totally different in daylight. A sea of tickets rippled along the ground, along with fliers and other rubbish. I hung around the entrance for a while, not knowing what to do. I wanted to go back in, wanted to experience that different world, but held back, a young nervous girl after all.

I saw one of the men from last night and started to wave and smile.

He turned to me, staring blankly and I realised my mistake. Despite looking similar, he was a stranger. My hand dropped along with my smile. I stood there, wondering if I should turn and run when I heard a familiar voice shout out 'Well hello little miss!'

Appearing from behind that first stranger was one of the Irish from last night, broad grin threatening to split his pale face. In the day light, his skin was so white it was almost translucent, blue even. He walked over and we started chatting as though we'd been friends all our lives. He took me gently by the elbow and led me into the circus. We strolled through the circus, and others from last night joined us. They had a similar look, even their mannerisms were the same. All walked with quick, agile movements, making next to no footprints. They greeted each other and welcomed me.

We met others in the circus. The black woman was there, dressed in sensible, manly clothes. Next to her walked a tall man, also black with the greenest eyes. They smiled at me, and went on their way.

The old Chinese man shuffled past, grunting a 'How do' in an accent that most certainly wasn't Chinese. His three attendants trailed behind him, giggling and hiding their smiles with fans. All three stared curiously and unashamedly at me, and I stared back, not used to seeing such beauty. In unison, they bowed their heads, giggled again, and ran off to catch up with the old man.

As the day wore on, I realised I hadn't seen or heard a single animal.

My group (as I was already starting to think of them) invited me to lunch and we shared a simple but delicious meal under the shade of a canvas roof. Sitting there, I spotted the old guitarist. He sat alone, and there was the only animal I saw. The old monkey and he ate from the same plate. He broke bread and gave small chunks to the monkey who sat patiently next to him. Other than that, I saw no other creature.

'So, you came back,' came the thick accented voice of the ringmaster behind me. I jumped at the sound of his voice, and cursed myself for blushing yet again.
He was accompanied by his friend from the night before, and she was even more beautiful than I

remembered. She looked at me with large eyes, staring intently before breaking into a wide smile.

'We knew you'd be back,' she said, her accent matching his, 'and you are most welcome. We are, after all, family.'

The two of them sauntered off, stopping to greet others. They sat down next to the old man, and spent the rest of their lunch with him.

As for me, I hung around with the others until it was getting close to opening time. People started to pile in again, and the circus folk got busy. I hung back for a bit and eventually drifted off home alone. As I walked back through the corn fields, crows kept me company, cawing at each other in the dim light.

I returned the next day and it was then that I made up my mind. I all but ran home, going through several imagined conversations with

Grandma. She sat on the porch as I slowed down, catching my breath and mind in one go.

‘Grandma…’ I started, ‘I…erm’

‘I know, my little princess’, she replied before I could even get a complete sentence out.

‘You go. You will always have a place to roost here if need be. Go now, before you change your mind.’

I think I kissed her then, her soft cheeks like paper, smelling like the soap she bought in bulk at the drugstore. I went upstairs to change.

When I came down again, Grandma was waiting for me with a smile.

‘Oh my angel’, she sighed, ‘You look just like your mother.’

She stroked my feathers, fingers lingering on the tips, and kissed my beak. I let myself be held until she was ready to let me go. And with that, I flew out the window and was gone.

ACKNOWLEDGEMENTS

This book could never have happened without the help of quite a few people. First and foremost, the support of both my wife and daughter has kept me going. They have listened to my ideas, given feedback and have always encouraged me to keep on. So they are either to blame or to be thanked, depending on your point of view.

Second, I need to thank Dave Noble. He handed me a screenplay a while back and said 'You can use this if you want'. From that screenplay emerged the story 'Balls'. You might have noticed the brothers are Dave and Paul. It was my way of thanking him (and his brother). It's still one of my favourite stories, so thanks Dave!

Third, this book wouldn't look quite as snazzy if it wasn't for Marcus. I don't know if he understood just how much help I needed when I asked for some advice, but he's been an absolute trooper—

working on cover design, layout, suggesting content and even playing guitar.

Finally, it goes without saying, thanks to all the Kickstarter backers who have chipped in to make this happen. But I've just said it. So thank you all! I hope you all have enjoyed this book.

Who knows, maybe I'll write some more one of these days.

Printed in Poland
by Amazon Fulfillment
Poland Sp. z o.o., Wrocław